A QUILT DETECTIVE MYSTERY

A PATCHWORK
OF
POISON

A Mystery in 40 Motifs

KAREN LOWE

BEANPOLE BOOKS
www.beanpolebooks.co.uk

First edition
Published October 2012

Cover photo by Barry Lowe

www.beanpolebooks.co.uk

For Barry, Tom and Gemma
and for my mum

Born in Gower, South Wales, Karen Lowe moved to Shropshire when she was five. After graduating in London with a BA in French, German and English Literature, she worked as a secretary in Fleet Street and the West End. She returned to Shropshire with her land surveyor husband to bring up their two children, and worked for Shropshire Libraries before training in garden design.

Her children's stories were broadcast on BBC TV's *Play School*, and her collection of Shropshire folk stories, *Witches & Warriors: Legends from the Shropshire Marches*, was published by Shropshire Books.

She published a series of crossword books on Shropshire, Gardening, and Literature under her imprint Beanpole Books and in 2005 published her first crime novel, *Death in the Physic Garden* introducing garden designer Fern Green. It had taken ten years to write. The sequel, *Death in the Winter Garden*, published in 2010, took a mere seven years to complete. *The Quilt Detective: a Patchwork of Poison* is her first crafting murder mystery, inspired by her love of creative textiles.

www.karenlowe.co.uk

1

BRON

'Them quilts, how much are they worth then?'

The girl's voice made me jump. I hadn't heard anyone follow me out of the lecture hall. I glanced round, trying to balance the box of slides and fabrics as I pressed the car remote.

'Depends on the quilt,' I said.

I had just given a talk on the history of quilts, with slides, to the Women's Institute. The girl did not look as if she belonged to the WI. Late teens, pierced nose and eyebrow, Goth make-up, she wore a black studded leather jacket, a strip of black leather skirt over thick black tights, her feet strapped and buckled into sturdy Doc Martens. Not the most comfortable combination for a warm May evening.

'Could you …?' I nodded towards the boot of the muddy Land Rover. She opened the door for me. 'Thanks. Were you at the talk? I didn't see you,' I said.

'I was in the kitchen.'

'You're into quilting, then?'

The girl's spider-lashed eyes narrowed with contempt.

'No way.'

'It's not all log cabins and satin stitch. You've seen Tracey Emin's take on quilting?'

She shook her head impatiently. 'Here,' she said. Her glossy black fingernails were curled around a mobile phone. On the small screen was a photo of a patchwork quilt: a honeycomb of embroidered pinks,

5

greens and creams, exquisitely pretty.

'How much is it worth?' she prompted.

'It depends,' I told her. 'The age of the quilt, its condition, the fabrics used, the craftsmanship, and of course its provenance.' She stared dully at me from under her straight black fringe. 'Where it comes from,' I said. 'Do you know anything about its history?'

'It was my great-grandma's,' she said, pushing the phone back into the pocket of her jacket. 'She said I was to have it when she died.'

'Surely you don't want to sell it?'

'Why not? If it'll get me out of this dump.'

I gave a sigh of disappointment. So it wasn't curiosity about textile art and its history that had brought the girl here after all. Just the lure of bright lights, the yearning to be 'somewhere else'. I could just about remember what that was like.

'If it's a valuation you want, you'd do better to take it to an auction house,' I told her. 'They'll have experts to advise you.'

'But you know about quilts. The history, an' all that,' the girl persisted. 'You're the quilt detective.'

The hint of desperation in her tone made me hesitate. With the picture of the quilt in my mind, and that tremor of vulnerability in her voice, it wasn't easy just to walk away. Wouldn't do any harm to try and help, would it? Might even convert the girl to quilting.

'All right,' I relented. 'I'll do my best. But I'll need to see the quilt for myself.'

'Tomorrow,' the girl said, backing away. 'I'll bring it to you tomorrow.'

'You don't know where I live,' I said but already the girl was striding across the car park. Of course, these days, it wasn't hard to track anyone down. She'd just Google 'Bronwen Jones' to find my website and contact information. According to the website I was a 'textile artist'. Now it seemed I had a second profession: quilt detective.

'Well, it's your own fault,' I told myself. Wasn't that how I'd structured my talk that evening? Every quilt had a story. It was just a matter of teasing it out from the scraps of fabric, the painstaking stitches. Unlocking its secrets.

As I started the car, I felt a tingle of excitement. Tomorrow I'd get to see that beautiful quilt for real.

Tuesday

From its hillside perch above Bishops Castle, Ceri Cottage had a perfect view of the gentle hills and wooded slopes of the Welsh borderland. Behind the cottage, the fifteen miles of the ancient Kerry Ridgeway led westward into Wales. It was both peaceful and invigorating, for though the hills still bore reminders of the past: Iron Age tumuli, standing stones, ditches and castle mounds, it was totally untainted by reminders of my old life in Surrey with Ed. At Ceri Cottage I was free to indulge my love of fabric, texture, colour, and pursue the career I'd dreamed of for so long; a career I'd put on hold while we built up his landscaping business together. Free to sew, paint, dabble and do whatever I pleased, without having to plan around Ed's working day, the timetable of accounts and invoices, the estimates and ordering, the tyranny of the telephone, and the succession of demanding and hopelessly unrealistic clients.

Swan's feet: that's how I thought of my life with Ed. The swan's graceful progress across the lake is only possible because of its powerful feet thrashing away out of sight below the surface. Ed had been the one doing

7

all the gliding in our lives.

I made coffee and ate the last wedge of carrot cake. From my studio window, I watched two hikers with rucksacks stride past the low wall of the cottage garden. Would the girl really bring the quilt to show me?

'Just as well if she doesn't,' I thought. I didn't need any distractions. I had an exhibition to prepare for. Clive Rednal was taking a risk allowing me space in his gallery, and in July too. As he never ceased to remind me. Followed by his swift assurance that 'I know you'll sell really well, Bron'.

I pressed my foot down on the sewing machine pedal and imagined it was Clive's throat. I guided the fabric under the needle, creating swirling black trails of veins along the stretch of dyed brown calico that would become tree bark in an art quilt to team with the already finished leafy profusion of '*Summer*' and the stark branches of '*Winter*'. Just one more season to go then.

By four, I'd had enough of leaves. Stretching my arms, I rubbed the nape of my neck. My shoulders ached from sitting bent over my sewing all afternoon, hand-stitching the coppery scraps of silk cut into leaf shapes, embroidering a tracery of veins and spines. I heard a noise in the kitchen. At the studio door stood the girl, dressed head to toe in black again.

'I brought you the quilt,' she said, shrugging the rucksack from her shoulder.

'Good. Let's have a look then.' I smiled and tried not to show she'd made me jump. Again. Tried not to look too keen, either. Didn't want to frighten her away. Just because I'd been waiting all day for her to show up with the quilt.

The girl's glance slid past me, taking in the front room of the cottage that I'd made my studio, the distracting view of fields and hills through the bay window. Fabric scraps spilled from teetering piles of bags and boxes, a length of undyed calico draped the table beside my sewing machine. The chimney breast was flanked with shelves sagging under their burden of books and paints, and a magpie collection of lace scraps, buttons and beads. On the opposite wall I'd pinned up black and white enlargements of my photos of deeply veined and corded tree bark, tangling roots. Beside them hung the two finished quilts in patchwork, shaded through greens, cream, terracotta and brown, and layered with corded cotton and silk threads that mimicked the tree bark.

'That yours?' the girl said.

I nodded. 'The green leafy one's '*Summer*'. The other's '*Winter*'. They're based on the old chestnut trees at Croft Castle. I've got an exhibition in July at the Rednal Gallery in Ludlow.'

'I hate trees,' she said. 'Give me the creeps.'

She retreated into the kitchen diner, dumped her rucksack on the table. In black jeans and a black t-shirt with a sequinned dragon, she looked smaller, and thinner, than I remembered.

'I was just about to make some tea,' I said. 'Sorry there's no cake left.'

The French doors were still slightly open where the girl had let herself in. I could feel the draught. A fickle month, May. Warm sunshine yet there was still the threat of a late frost. My birth month, and a forty-second birthday that had passed without fanfare. I noticed the crumbs of mud by the computer desk in the corner. The girl's black boots were mud-rimmed. How long had she been there, snooping round?

'So what do I call you?' I handed her a mug of tea.

'Cat,' she said. 'Short for Caitlin.' She opened the rucksack and hauled out a plump carrier bag. Inside was a bundle of pink fabric. She unfolded it, turning it over to reveal the gentle colours of the quilt, its small hexagons embroidered with leaves and flowers. I let out a soft sigh. You just couldn't tell from a photo.

'It's like a garden,' I said. Some four foot square, the small interlocking hexagons were exquisitely decorated. I recognised daisies, an oak leaf, a key. It was beautiful. Quilts were often made by young women for their marriage bed or for a baby's cot. Something to be treasured rather than used for everyday. Usually the quilt would have been lined with wool or felt, perhaps an old blanket, then backed with a matching fabric and the three layers sewn together with a quilting pattern, but it seemed the quilt top had been left incomplete. Beautiful though it was, the pink flowery backing fabric was a more recent Laura Ashley print, stitched to the top in hurried uneven stitches. It would detract from its value. 'So it was your great-grandmother's?'

Cat nodded. 'It's really ancient, see?' She pointed to the corner hexagon. There was a date neatly embroidered: 1881. And the initials *HD*. 'My great-grandma put a new lining to it. She'd some material left over from her curtains so she wanted it to match. It was her grandmother who made the quilt. She was called Harriet. Don't know what the 'D' stands for. Maybe you could find out. Do some detective work.'

'I could try,' I said. 'It's a really beautiful quilt top.'

'Two grand.'

'What?'

'That's how much I need,' Cat said. 'You said it was beautiful.'

'You'd be lucky to get two hundred,' I said. She looked disappointed. 'But I told you, you'll get a better idea of value from an auction house. Anyway, why do you need so much money?' I only just stopped myself adding, 'at your age'. I'm beginning to sound like my mother, I thought. I was old enough to qualify, I realised dejectedly.

'I'm going travelling. Getting away from here,' she said, defiant.

'But a quilt like this … it's your inheritance … you can't just sell it.'

'Why not? My life, isn't it?'

'Besides, you're very young to go travelling on your own.'

The girl rolled her eyes. 'I'm eighteen,' she said. The tilt of her head, the challenge in her eyes, suggested she had practised that line a time or two with barmen and club bouncers. It didn't convince me either.

'Sorry. I can't help you,' I said, returning her stare, my hands tightly clasped, away from the irresistible quilt. If the girl wasn't going to tell me the truth, I didn't want to get involved, no matter how beautiful the quilt was, nor how sorely its history tempted me.

Cat scraped back her chair and got to her feet. Rolling up the quilt she began stuffing it back in her rucksack.

'Where are you going?'

'What do you care?'

That desperate look flickered again in the girl's eyes. I felt guilty then. I'd promised to help. I was supposed to be the grown-up here, patient and mature, though as a Gemini, patience and maturity were not my strongest suits.

'Look, why don't you finish your tea and tell me a bit more about the quilt,' I coaxed.

11

Cat glanced out to the garden, to freedom.

'Cat?' I touched the girl's arm. Saw her flinch. Saw the bruises then on her wrists, as she hoisted the rucksack onto her shoulder. 'What happened?' I demanded.

'Nothing.'

'You asked for my help.'

'With the quilt,' she snapped. 'Don't try telling me what to do.'

'As if,' I said softly.

The girl's shoulders slumped a little, the wire-tense body relaxing. She turned back to the table.

'You got any biscuits?'

'My great-grandmother, Nanna Kate, told me the quilt had secrets in it,' Cat said. 'When she was a little girl, her grandma gave her the quilt and she told me about a big house and a fortune that should have been hers. She said to keep the quilt safe and one day it would make her rich. Never did though.' Her glance brightened. 'But maybe she's right. Maybe it's worth a fortune now.'

'It's a shame the quilt backing isn't original,' I said. 'The new stitching's very poorly done.'

'Wasn't my fault,' Cat muttered. 'It was that cow. My mum. Came back from school, and she's there on my bed, cutting the lining off the quilt. I screamed at her. Wasn't her quilt, was it? And she was spoiling it. It's money, she says. Listen, you can hear it. Old pound notes, she reckons. And you can. You can hear the paper crackling inside. Only it isn't money. It's just bits of paper. Hexagon shapes.'

'The pattern pieces,' I said. 'Paper was a real luxury. They'd use any scraps they could find. Bills, old letters, laundry lists. Nothing wasted. Useful for dating a quilt though,' I said more eagerly. 'That and the type of fabric. Not many of them have the date embroidered in the corner like this one. It's a good start.'

Cat sighed. 'I tried to fix it. I sewed the material back on again but it didn't look the same. She's ruined it. Like she ruins everything for me. I hate her. We had a bit of a fight. Not the first time,' she said, 'But this time, I'm not going back.'

'She'll be worried about you.'

'Fat chance!'

'And you should be at school.'

Cat shook her head. 'Study leave. Exams. Only I'm not doing them.'

'Why ever not? I bet you'll do well.'

'What's the point?' Cat said fiercely. 'I want to travel. I can get a job.'

'Easier if you've done the exams first,' I said.

'I just need some money. I've got to get away from here.'

'So you decided to sell the quilt.'

'Two hundred quid,' Cat said desperately. 'You said it was worth that at least. I can get to London. Find my dad. He'll help me.'

'Look, I'll do some detective work. Find out a bit more about the quilt. See what it's really worth. You can wait just a little while, can't you?'

'How long?" she said, suspicious.

'When do your exams start?'

'Two weeks. But I told you I'm not sticking around to do them.'

'You can stay here if you want.' As soon as I said it, I knew it was stupid. I was going to regret it. I had the exhibition to work for. Whatever would Clive say? 'But you have to tell your mother where you are.'

Cat snorted. But texted all the same. It was a truce of sorts. But I knew I hadn't won yet.

Patiently, cautiously, I began to snip at the large stitches Cat had sewn through the quilt in her effort to re-attach the quilt backing. I could hear the faint rustle of paper from inside the quilt, like voices murmuring, conspiring. As I lifted off the backing fabric, I could see the paper hexagons underneath, just as Cat had said. There was tiny spidery handwriting across some of the paper pieces, the ink a rusty brown. On others, there was the merest shadow of letters where the ink had long since faded. Not old pound notes, but valuable, just the same. A glimpse into another life, over a hundred years ago.

'What does it say?'

'Not sure. Could be old recipes. Pieces cut from someone's letters.'

'Love letters?' she said, peering closely.

'Maybe.'

'My great-great-great-grandmother's,' Cat said. 'Grandma Harriet.' Delicately she touched the tiny almost illegible script, written by a woman she had never known, a woman who was her own blood, her own family. 'No-one's seen this before. Not since she wrote it in 1881. How cool is that!'

'Except for your great-grandmother,' I reminded her. 'She replaced the lining. Didn't she say anything about the writing?'

Cat nodded. 'That's when she told me the quilt had a secret.'

'But she didn't tell you what it was?'

'Only what her grandma had told her when she was little. About the lost fortune.'

'It'll take a bit of working out exactly what she has written,' I said. 'We can start at one corner and work along. Not all of the pieces have anything written on them.'

I lifted the fold of tacked fabric and peered at the paper underneath.

'There's a name,' I said. 'It looks like *Cropstone Hall.*'

'I know where that is,' Cat said, frowning. 'It's a big house. Really posh.' She stared at the writing on the pattern piece. 'But what was Grandma Harriet doing there?' she said, puzzled. She glanced at me, her cheeks flushed. 'You reckon she was a lady? Maybe there really is a lost fortune!'

'She could have been in service there,' I said. 'When I researched my family history, they were mainly farm workers and domestic servants. But there is an easy way to find out what Harriet was doing at the Hall,' I said. 'We can try the online census records. There was a census every ten years. If we search for Cropstone Hall in 1881, it should show Harriet living there. And exactly what she was doing. And we'll find out her surname.'

'Lady Harriet,' Cat said dreamily. 'Perhaps there is money in that quilt after all. Perhaps it's proof of our long lost inheritance.'

I smiled. For the first time, the girl seemed relaxed. Happy, even. And she hadn't mentioned travelling for a good ten minutes. I bent over the quilt once more, trying to decipher the tiny curling handwriting, the faint shadows of script, teasing out the secrets of the quilt piece by piece. So I had two weeks to sort something out, with the girl's mother, with the school, with Cat herself. Time to persuade Cat that her exams were important, that it wouldn't hurt to put her travel plans on hold for a year or two, till she was older, wiser, less vulnerable. Fleetingly I imagined a graduation ceremony, applauding like mad as Cat stepped up to receive her degree. Her hugs and thanks, the tears. '*If you hadn't taken me under your roof that day ...*'

'What if it's worth more than two hundred?' Cat said excitedly, cutting into my daydreams. She span round on the computer chair, beaming. 'I can go to Peru!'

'There he is. William Dash. Widower. Landowner, Cropstone Hall,' I read out. Cat peered at the census page on the computer screen. 'And one daughter.'

'Harriet. That's her!' Cat said. 'Aged 16.' She sat back and stared at me. 'My age,' she said. 'Is that spooky or what?'

'Harriet Dash. I can just imagine her, sitting in the drawing room peacefully stitching the quilt for her marriage bed.'

'Widower, it says. Wonder what happened to her ma then,' Cat said, frowning.

'You could go back to the 1871 census. See if her mother was alive then,' I suggested, but as I reached for the mouse again, Cat stopped me.

'Look, there's a nurse. Gwen Lloyd, it looks like. Unmarried. Aged 31. You reckon Harriet was ill or something?'

'Nursemaid,' I said, deciphering the scrawl. 'She's Harriet's Nanny. She'd be the one looking after the girl, seeing to her clothes, her meals. Probably been with her since she was born. Likely Harriet was educated at home too.'

'Home schooling. Poor kid. Bet she had no mates then. And look at all those servants. There's a pageful: housekeeper, cook, domestic servants, gardeners, groom. All of them just to look after her and her dad. She'd never have to wash up or tidy her room.'

'But there wasn't much choice for her apart from marriage.'

'You ever been married?' Cat asked.

'I don't want to talk about it,' I said crisply.

'Oooh. Cheat on you, did he?'

'I told you,' I warned her. Right now, I had no wish to remember what had happened. Some doors were best kept firmly closed.

'All right, all right, I only asked,' Cat said, hands held up in surrender. 'So you've got no kids then?'

'No, no children.' I got noisily to my feet. 'I'd better make some dinner. You hungry?'

Cat nodded, her attention already refocused on the census page. She pressed the print button.

'Wonder who Harriet married. Some rich bloke with a country house I expect. So who got all her money?'

'Her husband of course. She was his property. If you want, you can look in the marriage registers. It'll give two brides and two grooms per page. Shouldn't be hard to work out which one she married if we crosscheck with the census returns.'

'I want to find her ma first. You reckon she died when Harriet was born? They often did, didn't they? I'll try the 1871 census first. She's my great-great … well, lots of greats grandmother. I'd love to know who she was.'

I chopped up some onions and mushrooms and found a packet of risotto rice. I peered into the fridge, vainly hoping to find something to go with it. I stirred the stock with the rice in the pan, and cut up wedges of French bread. Tossed a bowlful of salad leaves from the garden, and sprinkled on some herbs and a little grated parmesan.

'I found her!' Cat said. 'In 1871 she was alive and well. Eleanor Dash. Wife. Aged 32. And little Harriet just six years old. And there's her nursery maid, Gwen Lloyd, aged 21. How cool is that! I've found my great-great-great-great-grandma. Eleanor Dash, of Cropstone Hall. Wonder when she died.'

'You can try the FreeBMD website later. That lists all the births, deaths and marriages registered in England since 1837. Come and eat.'

'Poor Harriet. I know me and mum hate each other at times, but to think she didn't have a ma when she was my age.'

'Maybe she did die in childbirth,' I said. 'She was young enough to have more children after Harriet. Perhaps the baby died with her.'

'That's really sad,' Cat said. She sat down at the kitchen table and reached for the bread. 'I'm never having kids.'

'I'm sure, if you meet the right man, you'll change your mind.'

'You didn't,' Cat said.

I glared at her. 'I told you …'

'Anyway, I'm not getting married. Never.' There was defiance in Cat's stare that mirrored mine. Had she already had her heart broken by someone? Was that why she was so anxious to get away from home? 'None of your business,' I told myself. Though it might make for an awkward couple of weeks, tiptoeing around each other's feelings. Too late to change my mind now. I'd promised Cat she could stay and that was that.

Once Cat had found her way around the websites she needed, I left her to follow the trail of her research. I cleared the dishes, then carefully finished unpicking the backing from Cat's quilt. Gently I smoothed my fingers over the thin rumpled paper pieces. Where to start unravelling their story?

'I can't find her,' Cat said, a bleak disappointment in her voice.

'Who?'

'Harriet. She's not on the 1891 census anywhere. And she's not married. Least, I tried that site, like you said, but it's not matched her up with anyone.'

'Maybe she went abroad. A lot did. Travelled out to some far-flung corner of the Empire to marry. She must be somewhere. She must have had a child, else you wouldn't be here, would you?'

'No. Course not,' Cat said, brightening. 'India. I reckon she went out to India. My mum always wanted to go. My nan went, before mum was born. The hippy trail, she called it. That's where she met my grand-dad. Only they never married or anything. He just went on travelling.'

'Perhaps there'll be a clue in the quilt as to what happened to Harriet. A piece from a love letter maybe. There's nothing on the next piece, and I can't make out the writing on the next one, it's faded too much. Oh …'

'What is it?'

'The writing … the letters look the wrong way round.'

'Like mirror writing? We used to do that, and invisible ink. You do it in lemon juice then you have to heat it to read it.'

'I don't think it's mirror writing,' I said, reaching for the scissors. Delicately I snipped through the tacking stitches that held the fabric folded over the paper. I drew out the flimsy paper and turned it over. Across the centre were the pale lines of writing that had shown through so faintly on the reverse.

'What is it?' Cat breathed, pressing closer for a better view.

'Looks like part of a diary. '*April 19th*' it says.'

'You reckon that's what this is? Harriet's secret diary?'

'I don't suppose there'd have been much privacy in a house full of servants. It's a good way of hiding your thoughts, stitching them where they couldn't be seen.' I replaced the pattern piece on the fabric.

'We can unpick each hexagon and copy out what she's written,' Cat said eagerly.

'I don't want to risk spoiling the quilt. You have to respect its heritage too.'

'My heritage,' Cat said, that stubborn look in her eyes that I was beginning to recognise only too well. 'I want to know what Harriet Dash was hiding. All these years we could have been entitled to a fortune we never even knew about. I have to know what she says.'

I peered closely at the words, in that tiny curling script. '*Tuesday 19th April. She came today. Catherine Pendine.*'

Cat bent to read for herself. '*Catherine Pendine*', she read aloud. '*I mean to …*'

'*I mean to find out all about her,*' I finished for her.

Cat glanced up. 'Doesn't sound too happy, does she?'

'It said the 1881 census was taken on the night of 3rd April. Catherine Pendine isn't at the house then. Harriet is living there with her nursemaid Gwen Lloyd. But soon after that, Harriet begins her secret diary.'

'Wonder where Catherine Pendine was on the 3rd April. And what happened to her,' Cat said, retreating to the computer, munching the last of the bread. For someone so slender, she had quite an appetite.

I made up a bed for her on the couch beside the computer and left her to her online research.

'Make sure you get some sleep. I don't want to come down in the morning and find you slumped over the keyboard,' I told her. 'Having QWERTY imprinted on your forehead is not a good look.'

'Promise,' Cat said distantly, already engrossed in her hunt for Catherine Pendine.

I folded up the patchwork quilt and put it on a shelf in the studio, yet it was some time before I fell asleep. Ed was the problem. Hadn't he always been? Well, at least for the past five years. Telling Cat glibly, '*If you meet the right man, you'll change your mind,*' had not been the whole truth. I thought I had met the right man. Trouble is, I wasn't the right woman. We'd made a good team, though. We'd planned to work hard and build up the landscaping business before I could step back and develop a career of my own, before we had children. I always thought that was what we'd agreed. But I was wrong. As I discovered one day when I happened to see her, a former client of ours, very pretty, very slim, and very pregnant. What I'd been planning and working for had not been what Ed had in mind at all. When the baby was born, he left for good. That was over three years ago. It had cost him, of course. He'd had to buy my share of the business. We sold the house and split the money. It was more than enough to buy and convert a cottage a hundred miles away. Enough for me to live on, carefully, while I whole-heartedly pursued a career in textile art. I enjoyed my new life, I felt comfortable. And had put on half a stone a year ever since to prove it. And some days I didn't miss Ed at all. But there were few days I didn't think of him.

*

21

It was late when I woke. With a start I remembered my guest.

'Cat!'

All was quiet downstairs. Teenagers. Of course Cat would still be fast asleep on the couch. I wondered how far along her family tree she'd managed to get. And looked forward to uncovering more of the little paper hexagons with their secret diary.

'Morning, sleepyhead,' I said, padding into the kitchen. But the couch was empty, the sheets and duvet neatly folded. I went into the studio, my heartbeat quickening, and turned to the shelf. The quilt was gone. I felt for a moment a pang of dismay. And then I saw it, folded neatly on the table by the sewing machine. Relief flooded through me. Absurd. The quilt wasn't even mine. There was a note on top of it, printed on a hexagon cut from my notepad.

'Need to do more research.' She'd signed it with the squiggled image of a cat.

Research, but where? The local studies library in Ludlow? I wished I'd taken a note of Cat's mobile number. I was meeting Clive in Ludlow at twelve. I could have given Cat a lift back.

I grilled the last of the smoked bacon, made tea and toast spread with fragrant chunky marmalade. Beside the computer were the census printouts, and Cat's scribbles as she had tried to piece together her family tree. I skimmed down the census page for Cropstone Hall 1871: William and Eleanor Dash, Cat's four times great-grandparents, and their only daughter, Harriet. Was there really a lost fortune? It was intriguing. I just hoped Cat wasn't going to be disappointed.

On my way into Ludlow to meet Clive Rednal, I stopped off at the library. There was no sign of Cat and the staff couldn't be sure they had seen her. They were certain no-one had enquired about Cropstone Hall that day. Half an hour later I emerged with a potted history. A Georgian house, Grade 2 listed, built in the early 1800s for the Dash family, merchants of Ludlow, and sold in 1900 after the death of William Dash. Of the heirs to his estate there was no mention. Whoever Harriet had married must have had property of their own. Or '*some rich bloke*', as Cat had put it.

The Rednal Gallery was in a converted stable block in a courtyard behind the market square in Ludlow. Through the large plate glass window I could see Clive giving directions to his latest assistant, a slender six-foot blonde-haired Russian girl, Irena, who had a passion for Art Deco. She was hanging a small canvas on the back wall. Judging from her expression, it was not one she admired.

'Bron, my favourite artist,' Clive came across the room and hugged me, kissing both cheeks. 'How are the quilts coming along?' he asked anxiously.

'They're growing,' I assured him. Today he was wearing a blue cotton shirt that he no doubt knew made his blue eyes all the more dazzling, and set off his unseasonally tanned complexion.

'I don't want to be blamed for keeping you from your work,' he said sternly.

'Even starving artists have to eat sometimes.'

He gave a rumbling laugh. OK, so the baggy silk shirt I wore over loose linen trousers did not entirely conceal the truth. I knew I didn't look as if I often went without food. But I was hungry.

'Lunch, Irena. Back in an hour,' he called as Irena tottered up the stairs on high spiky heels, her long slim legs in tight black trousers, her white silk shirt belted round a handspan waist.

'Enjoy,' she said with a flash of smile from glossy scarlet lips. She didn't look as if she ate more than birdseed.

Clive headed across the courtyard to the bistro and took the table by the window.

'Seriously, it is all coming along on schedule, isn't it?' he asked as I sipped a glass of chilled Chenin Blanc.

'Don't worry. I told you. I'll have the four major pieces finished by the end of June. The smaller pieces are all ready to hang.' I decided not to tell him about Cat and the patchwork quilt. He might not be in favour of the distraction. 'How's the current exhibition going?'

'Very safe. Very steady. Irena hates it.'

'I gathered.'

'She has good taste, that girl.'

'Maybe you should listen to her then.'

'I listen to my bank manager, my accountant, and my ex-wife. Not necessarily in that order,' he said. 'I know whose tune I need to dance to.'

'How is Caroline?'

'Blooming. She's just discovered gardening. If I didn't already know the answer, I'd ask you if you knew a good landscape gardener.'

I glared at him. Ed was off limits for polite conversation.

'Sorry.' He reached across the table and squeezed my hand. 'You're all right, though? Not too lonely up there in your country idyll.'

'I thought you wanted me to focus. No distractions,' I said.

24

'Quite right. All the same... if you did pine for a little company ...'

'Thank you, Clive. I'll bear it in mind.' I tried not to be flattered. I doubted he felt any real attraction to me. It was just habit. Clive was confident that, even at fifty-something, his broad-shouldered, Viking-like build and blue-eyed good looks were still as attractive to women as they had always been. Not without reason.

As Clive ordered our salmon quiche and new potato salad, I watched the straggle of lunchtime shoppers pass the window. I hoped, for Clive's sake as much as my own, that July would be a busy month.

'Cat?' It was just a glimpse as the girl hurried past the window, but I recognised that sequinned dragon t-shirt, the Doc Martens, the black hair. 'Sorry, Clive, there's someone I must see ...'

'But I've just ordered,' Clive protested.

'It'll only take a minute.'

I headed out of the bistro, through the courtyard, out into the bustle of midday shoppers in the market square, weaving round the army of pushchairs. Where had she gone? I stood, puffing and hot, in the midst of the busy market. Then I caught sight of her, under the awning of one of the stalls. She was looking at silver jewellery.

'Cat!'

The girl did not hear me above the noise of traffic and people. As she turned away from the stall, I caught her arm.

'Cat ...'

But the girl who turned round, mouthing an oath, was not Cat. Same dark hair, same eyelashes, but taller, a little plumper.

'What the 'ell do you want?' she demanded.

'Oh. Sorry. I thought … I thought you were someone else.' I let go of her, my face burning.

She glared at me, muttering obscenities.

She had to be about the same age though, didn't she? Same taste in fashion. At the same school, maybe?

'I'm a friend of Cat's. Caitlin …' I said as she turned away. 'She's at school here. She's got a t-shirt like yours. Do you know her?'

She glanced back at me: the same defensive stare, the narrowed eyes.

'What if I do?'

'She came to see me yesterday. Stayed the night, and then this morning she'd gone. I don't have her phone number. I just wanted to make sure she was OK.'

'It's the anniversary, ain't it?' she said with impatience.

'Anniversary?'

'I thought you said you knew her,' the girl said, accusing, suspicion glinting in those narrowed eyes.

'I do. Of course I do.'

'Well then, you'd know,' she said.

'Obviously I don't. She didn't tell me everything. But I know she wanted to get away from here, just as soon as she could.'

'Yeh, that's Cat all right,' the girl conceded.

'Look, in case you do see her, would you give her my phone number?' I dug a business card out of my bag and handed it to her. She took it gingerly, studied it, then slipped it into the pocket of her jacket with a curt nod.

'I'm Nicky. Nicky Price,' she said. She studied me a moment, head tilted to one side. 'It was a year ago. He hanged himself in the woods,' she said. 'Ben Thomas. They were best mates, him and Cat. Never thought he'd do something like that.'

'Thanks …' I said bleakly, though the girl was already threading her way rapidly between the shoppers. A boy hanged in the woods. A year ago. Alarm began drumming in my head. So where had Cat gone? Was she all right? Was that why she didn't want to go in for her exams, because of what had happened to Ben?

'*I hate trees*,' she had said. '*Give me the creeps.*' Now I knew why.

'Cat, where are you?' It wasn't just the patchwork quilt that was a mystery.

2

HARRIET
1881

'No, no, no!' It could not be. And yet she knew there was nothing she could do to change her father's decision.

'I've hired a finishing governess for you, Harriet,' he had informed her that morning. 'Your nanny is going to a new post in Ludlow after Easter. Your aunt has need of a good nursery maid.'

'No!'

A sudden gust snatched off her bonnet and sent it bowling along the muddy ruts of the track. Harriet set off in pursuit along the ridgeway.

The horseman reined back hard as he caught sight of her: a froth of lace-edged petticoats, buttoned boots, a neat waisted jacket, and a tumble of auburn curls and velvet ribbons. Harriet span round at the sound of hoof beats. She saw the silhouette of horse and rider rear against the sun's glare.

'My bonnet! Watch where you're going!' she cried out.

She saw his lips widen in a wolf-like smile. Iron-grey eyes glinted beneath thick dark brows. Then, with a kick of his heels to the horse's flanks, he cantered on past her, scuffing up a shower of mud, his laughter gusting on the March wind. She glared after him, clutching her ruined bonnet, her heart pounding with indignation.

*

'Miss Harriet, look at the state of you! Your boots ... your hair!' Gwen scurried to meet her, her skirts and apron flapping like a hen rustling its feathers. Her broad face was pinched with disapproval, her fingers fluttering as she vainly tried to straighten ribbons, fasten buttons. The hem of the girl's skirt was caked with mud. 'She's here,' she said. 'Your Papa's been asking for you this past hour, and you out walking Lord knows where! You must go to him at once.'

'He can wait,' Harriet told her, and fled upstairs to her room.

'So what's she like?' Harriet asked as Gwen came in to help her change her skirt.

'As you'd expect. Ladylike, neatly dressed, but no money. Not if her gloves and boots are anything to go by,' Gwen said, her lips pursing. 'Learn what you can from her and please your Papa.'

'I don't want you to go,' Harriet told her. She could feel the tears begin to prickle again at her eyes. Why did Gwen have to go, just because of the governess's arrival?

'It's all settled,' Gwen said. 'You have to think of your future. And I must think of mine. I can't teach you French, nor how to play the piano, or how to dance at those fancy balls you'll be invited to.' Harriet caught her apprehensive glance in the mirror. 'You'll soon find a handsome young husband and have a grand house all of your own.'

'I don't want a husband,' she said. 'I want to stay here with you.'

Gwen gave a short sigh, the brush twisting in the girl's hair. From her look, Harriet knew she wasn't the only one who wanted to stay. But Gwen's duty was done, and there was an end on it. 'Ludlow's not far. And your dear aunt is a kind lady. You can come and visit if you've a mind to. Though I dare say you'll soon forget your old nanny once you've a string of suitors dancing to your tune.' She stepped back to admire her handiwork. 'There now. You'll do.'

'You asked to see me, Papa?'

Harriet closed the library door and waited, demure in dove-grey, hair brushed and pinned into submission, her cheeks rebelliously pink.

Her father stood by the window. The shutters, she noticed, had been folded back so that his tall wiry frame was swathed in sunlight. Five years they had been half closed, since the day her mother had died.

She sat stiffly on the edge of the ladder-back chair beside his desk, and kept her head bowed, staring instead at the two liver and white setters that dozed before the fire. Only the twitch of an ear, the flick of an amber eye belied their apparent indifference. She hated the dogs, his constant companions. Her father cared more about his dogs and his horses than he ever did about her. He had always wanted a son. Someone to inherit. She was a poor substitute.

'I hope you will profit from your studies with Miss Pendine,' he said sternly.

'Miss Pendine?' she enquired mildly. She glanced up at him and saw with satisfaction how his cheeks reddened with annoyance.

'Your new governess,' he said sharply.

There came the lightest of knocks on the door. She did not look round but heard the light tread, and could smell a faint perfume of roses and cloves. So this was Catherine Pendine, the woman who was to take Gwen's place.

She was slender, plainly dressed in a gown of dark grey trimmed with a cream lace collar. A pale complexion. Eyes of an icy blue that sparkled like frost on a winter morning. Quite without warmth.

'Harriet … I'm pleased to meet you,' she said in a voice that was soft and low like a dove's cooing.

'Miss Pendine.' Harriet gave a stiff nod of greeting. The governess moved past her, stirring the dust motes of the stuffy library with the swirl of her skirts, the wisp of her fragrance.

'If I may, I should like to show you my programme of lessons for Harriet, Sir,' she said. 'Once I've assessed Harriet's accomplishments, I may find there is a need for additional tutors.'

'As you see fit,' he answered, retreating to the window. 'I trust you to complete my daughter's education in a satisfactory manner and make up for the shortcomings in her temperament. I am sure we both wish for a successful conclusion.'

'I'm sure you won't be disappointed.' She glanced back at the girl with a bright smile. Harriet detected just the slightest tremor in her lips. A moment of self-doubt. Perhaps Miss Pendine was not as confident of her success as she pretended. And Harriet certainly had no intention of making her task an easy one.

Harriet closed her bedroom door and flopped heavily into the chair by the window. So that was it. It was not her education or her happiness that concerned her father: only that she should be married off, and swiftly, so that he could spend his time with his horses and his books uninterrupted. She glared across the peaceful parkland, the pewter mirror of the lake. Cropstone Hall no longer felt like her home.

She reached for her sewing box and drew out the scraps of silk and brocade from the tapestry bag. Her mother had always loved needlework. The quilts and cushions she had made were now all locked away in the chest in her room. If it hadn't been for Gwen, her walnut sewing box would have met the same fate. But Gwen had rescued it. As she turned the little brass key in its pearl lock, she could smell her mother's delicate lavender scent on the blue silk lining. She tucked the silver thimble onto her finger and reached for the heron-shaped scissors. Piecing together the scraps of fabric brought her some comfort, creating order out of the chaos after her mother's death. She found calm in the rhythm of stitching.

With compasses and ruler she drew a hexagon on an old haberdasher's bill and cut out the paper piece. Selecting a scrap of pale pink silk, she pinned the paper to it. She unwound a length of cotton, threaded a needle, and carefully, neatly, folded over the first edge of the silk and tacked it into place over the paper. But it was not her mother's face she saw as she stitched, but a pair of ice-blue eyes.

'I trust you to complete my daughter's education in a satisfactory manner and make up for the shortcomings in her temperament.' Her father's words stung as the needle pierced her skin. She sucked at the bead of blood. Again she carefully folded the next edge, stitching the layers of silk and paper together until the hexagon was complete and her temper had cooled.

'So what did you think of her?' Gwen asked as she brushed the girl's hair at the dressing table that evening. On the writing table by the window, her diary lay open, the few lines she had written were drying beneath the oil lamp's glow, her pen wiped clean and tucked back into the silver inkstand.

'I thought her rather dull,' Harriet said. She twisted round in her chair to better see Gwen's reaction. 'Who is she, Gwen? Who did she work for before?'

'Dear child, as if I'd know such things!' she said.

'Please, Gwenny,' she begged. 'Can't you find out?'

Gwen sighed and put down the silver-backed brush on the dressing table. She busied herself turning back the sheet and coverlet, plumping up the pillows. Harriet guessed she was working out how much to tell her. If she should tell her anything at all.

'All I know is that she was recommended by your father's lawyer,' she said at last.

'Mr. Adcott?' Harriet smiled then. If Gwen would tell her nothing, perhaps others could. 'Then I shall ask him about her when I come to Ludlow to visit you.'

Gwen's glance flew anxiously to the door as if afraid they were overheard. 'Come along, into bed with you. You'll have to arrange your visits with Miss Pendine now.'

Obediently Harriet slid beneath the covers. She reached up and hugged Gwen for the last time.

'Sleep well, my little one,' Gwen whispered. Her eyes shone, close to tears.

'I shall sleep very well,' Harriet told her. Gwen looked surprised by her calm. But Harriet was determined that the new governess's reign would be brief. She would have Gwen back. And already she had the first pieces in her patchwork puzzle: Catherine Pendine and lawyer Adcott. Who knows what shape the pattern would finally make?

Dinner, in the company of Catherine Pendine, was awkwardly silent. Usually her father took his meals in the library with his books and dogs for company, leaving Harriet and Gwen to eat together companionably in the schoolroom. But the arrival of the governess had changed even that long-standing arrangement. Her father joined them in the dining room.

Though of genteel background, as a governess Catherine Pendine was not considered to be a lady of the same standing as Harriet and her family, yet neither did she belong to the servant class. A place was set for her at the far end of the table, and she was served her meal after Harriet. And with a distinctly poorer helping, Catherine thought.

'I'll be away for a few days on business. I look forward to receiving news of Harriet's progress on my return,' William Dash announced.

'May I ask Purslow to take me to the station on Wednesday next?' Miss Pendine asked quickly. 'I have some affairs to conclude with Mr. Adcott in Ludlow.'

Harriet heard her father's gruff assent, but her attention was all on the governess. A visit to the lawyer. What business could she have with him? There was something almost desperate in the way she had asked.

With her duties completed for the day, Miss Pendine retired to her room after dinner. Mrs. Warren, the housekeeper, had given her Gwen's old room. 'As if she could ever replace her,' Harriet thought indignantly. She sat alone in the drawing room with her patchwork and embroidery silks, satin-stitching the petals of a pink rose, her mother's favourite flower, and a violet, symbol of watchfulness. Catherine Pendine had a secret, she was sure of it. If she could just discover it, she could be rid of her, and Gwen could come back.

When she returned to her bedroom that evening with her sewing box, Harriet could smell a faint rose scent in the room. She glanced to the table where she had been writing her diary before dinner: her first impression of Catherine Pendine, and the words, *'How long?'*

underlined. Had the governess come into her room and read her diary? She had need be more careful. She looked round for somewhere to hide her diary out of sight of prying eyes, and saw the sewing box, the little brass key still in the lock. Perfect. She lifted out the velvet-lined tray of needles, pins, and scissors, and tucked the diary underneath. She turned the key in the lock and hung it from a length of ribbon which she fastened round her neck for safekeeping. Tomorrow, she would start her search for the key to unlock Miss Pendine's secret.

French! What was the point of French? Harriet's lips tightened fiercely. However she tried, the words came out wrongly.

'Je suis, tu es …' It was all hopeless. She wanted to be outside, walking in the woods, or beside the lake, seeking plants for her botany studies. And she still had an hour of piano practice to endure.

'May I come with you tomorrow? To Ludlow?' she asked. 'I should like to visit my aunt and see that Gwen is settled into her new post.'

'I really don't think …'

'Aunt Isobel won't mind my visiting. She's been most kind to me since Mama …' Harriet faltered. 'And,' she said more brightly, 'I can practise French verbs on our journey.'

'Bien. D'accord,' Miss Pendine said, though her smile was strained.

The railway station at Horderley was but a short journey down the hill from the Hall. The little train brought them into Ludlow for mid-morning. Catherine Pendine delivered her charge safely to the Lindley's elegant town house off Ludlow's Castle Square.

'My business with Mr Adcott will require no more than an hour. I'll return for you then,' Miss Pendine told her.

With some impatience, Harriet greeted her aunt, and admired the three small Lindley children presented to her by a flustered Gwen.

'She's come to see Lawyer Adcott,' Harriet whispered to her nanny as tea was being poured. 'Catherine Pendine. She wouldn't tell me why. Have you found out anything about her?'

'Not a thing,' Gwen said.

'You must write to me and tell me any news you can discover,' Harriet instructed.

As soon as she could, she made her farewells and hurried along the street to the lawyer's office. Messrs Adcott & Probert were housed in a narrow three-storey building near St. Lawrence's Church. As Harriet turned the corner from the market place, she caught sight of Catherine Pendine on the steps of the lawyer's office. Clearly she was just entering the premises, though she had left Harriet at the Lindley's house some time ago. Where had she been? Almost at once she guessed the answer, for Miss Pendine, she realised, was not alone. There was a gentleman with her, in animated discussion, though at that distance, she could not make out what they said.

Harriet slipped back out of view into the doorway of the haberdashers, and waited till she judged the two had gone. As she emerged suddenly from hiding, she bumped straight into the very gentleman she had been avoiding.

'Forgive me, Madam,' he said hastily, and doffed his hat to her with an extravagant bow. As he straightened, his lips broadened with a smile.

Harriet recognised him at once. He was the man whose horse had trampled her bonnet on the ridgeway. She fixed him with her steeliest glare.

'Sir, you should look where you are going,' she said tartly, and hastened past him with crimsoning cheeks.

Robert Meredith stood watching after her for some little while, long after she had skipped up the steps into Lawyer Adcott's offices. A glimpse of a stockinged ankle, a flurry of lace. Yes, he knew exactly where he had seen her before. And he now had a very good idea who she was.

'Harriet ... I hope you haven't been waiting long.' Catherine Pendine emerged from Adcott's office looking distinctly flustered. Harriet turned her serene gaze from her governess to the elderly lawyer who came ponderously in her wake, his round eyes bulging in his fleshy crimson face.

'Aunt Isobel had another engagement,' Harriet told her blithely. 'It's only a few steps from her house to here.'

'Then we shall have time to look for a new bonnet for you before our train leaves,' the governess said.

As they passed through the outer office, a young clerk came in at the door, burdened by a pile of ledgers. He stared at Catherine then at Harriet, his lips gaping like a fish, then, blushing scarlet, pressed himself back against the wall for them to pass.

'Good-day, Samuel,' Catherine said with a warm smile. Harriet gave but the merest nod and marched on out into the street.

'Have you concluded your business with Lawyer Adcott?' she asked her governess as they made their way across the street to the milliners.

'Oh yes. All is in order now,' Catherine said calmly. Harriet wondered how at ease the governess would look if she told her she had seen her with the gentleman on the steps.

Was it a chance meeting? Had they planned to meet at that time, that day? Where had the governess been before going to the lawyer's office? She had certainly been anxious for permission to visit Ludlow that day. If she hadn't met the mystery gentleman, would he have come riding out to the Hall in search of her? Harriet paused from her diary page and gazed into the flicker of firelight. Was that what had brought him to the ridgeway that day? Was he looking for the governess? Who exactly was he? As she conjured his face again, she supposed he would be considered handsome. But what did Catherine Pendine think of him, she wondered? What was the link between them?

That evening as she snipped and stitched her patchwork pieces, she added another topic to her list. The identity of Miss Pendine's gentleman. A gentleman of means, judging by his fine horse, and his riding clothes. And, she realised, if Catherine Pendine were to marry him, she would be rid of her. And Gwen could come back.

The late April morning was warm, though the ragged grey clouds held a threat of showers. Harriet put on a light cloak over her gown and set out from the Hall equipped with her scissors and vasculum, the cylinder of tin into which she entrusted the plants she picked for her botany studies, its stout leather strap over her shoulder. Catherine Pendine, for once, did not insist on accompanying her. She had lessons to prepare, she said, their new French texts to study. Harriet walked briskly across the parkland and crossed the grassy bridge over the stream tumbling out from the lake. She paused to watch the cascading water. There were bright new fern fronds and plump cushions of moss starred with celandines. They would make a pleasing study, she thought, reaching to pluck some of the ferns to add to her collection. She nestled them safely in the damp cloth in the vasculum and closed the lid. Beyond the lake the ground rose up through woodland fringed with spiny hawthorn, the branches studded with pink tipped buds, where rosy chested bullfinches pecked.

She followed the path up through the woods towards the ridgeway track that meandered along the hill behind the house. The narrow stream rushed between steep mossy banks, splashing headlong towards the lake. Among the ferns on the bank grew clumps of primroses. She stooped to pick some, but as she straightened, she caught sight between the trees of a rider approaching. Her heartbeat quickened. Could it be Miss Pendine's gentleman again? He had not seen her yet. She turned back and hastily started down the path back to the Hall. Was that why the governess had not come with her that morning? Was she expecting him to call? Governesses were not usually permitted gentlemen callers, but in this case, Harriet decided, he should be encouraged. How delighted Gwen would be when she knew Miss Pendine had gone and she could come back to the Hall.

As the rider drew near, she could feel the drum of hoof beats vibrate through the hollow peaty earth. The horse slowed. She heard the chink of bridle, then the crack of twigs underfoot as the rider dismounted. She walked on, clutching tightly to the strap of the vasculum over her shoulder, not daring to stop or look round.

'Miss Dash. Forgive me. I know we have not been formally introduced …' he called after her. 'I owe you an apology. For the bonnet,' he said.

Her pace slowed. She could hear the horse's breath, the steady tramp of its hooves close behind her. Her heartbeat still seemed to throb in time with the thudding hoof beats.

'I'm Robert Meredith,' he introduced himself.

She glanced at him as he bowed, and saw his smile flicker on his lips like sunlight on the lake. His eyes were alive and merry, alert as a robin's, and she felt her former antipathy melt away. He was, she concluded, handsome, in a finely cut jacket and breeches, and leather riding boots that gleamed like chestnuts. More than a governess deserved. She lowered her gaze.

'It was a gust of wind took the bonnet, Sir. I don't blame you for that.'

'Then I am most relieved to hear it,' he said.

'I hope you have not ridden all this way for that apology?'

'It's an important mission,' he said. 'But not my only goal. I wanted to introduce myself to your father. I've newly come to the area. I was a friend of your late uncle in Hereford, William Watkins of Hopwood Hall.'

'Indeed? It is some time since we were at Hopwood,' she said. She felt a heat come into her face though the sun was not warming at all. She wished he would not gaze at her so intently, yet contrarily wished he would never look away. 'I'm sorry you've had a wasted journey. My father is away on business.'

He walked in step with her, leading his horse.

'You've been collecting plants?' he asked.

She glanced down at the vasculum.

'I … like to paint,' she said. 'I study botany.'

'A fascinating pastime,' he responded. 'And so rich a landscape too. It's well worth studying,' he said, his glance travelling across the parkland before returning to settle on her face. 'It is … very beautiful. Do you spend much time out here, studying?'

There was something in his look, in his words, that made her conscious that his admiration was not all for the landscape.

'Not as often as I would wish,' she said. 'Here's the Hall at last,' she said with some relief as they reached the grass bridge. She was trembling, she realised. What was she so afraid of? She was aware, with some satisfaction, that he had made no mention of her governess at all.

'May I leave my card with you, Miss Dash,' he said. 'For your father?'

She saw his gloved hand outstretched, holding his visiting card.

Robert Meredith Esquire. The name trilled through her with a melody all its own.

'Thank you, Mr. Meredith,' she said stiffly. 'I'm sure my father will be pleased to receive you, should you call again.'

'Good day to you, Miss Dash,' he said, his lips curling with that same soft smile, yet in his eyes as they sparkled, she read an amusement that seemed to delight at her discomfort.

She hurried away from him towards the Hall with no backward glance.

Harriet resolved to say nothing of their meeting to Catherine Pendine. She left the visiting card on her father's desk in the library. Her father would be back the following day. How soon would it be before Robert Meredith called again, she wondered?

41

'*Beautiful*,' he had said. Even now the memory of his words brought a heat to her cheeks. He had spoken with such admiration of the landscape. Indeed he had called her botanic studies '*fascinating*'. Had he really such a keen interest in botany? Her glance followed the familiar leather spines along the bookshelves. Reaching up from the library steps, she selected one of her favourites and carried the volume to the desk. Carefully she turned the thick pages. The flowers of meadow and hedgerow were exquisitely etched, the dog rose and violets hand-painted. It was then she remembered the primroses. She hurried back out to the hall. She had left the vasculum on the side table. The primroses must have wilted by now. Robert Meredith had quite put them out of her mind.

She opened the lid of the vasculum. The fragile primroses were limp and pale. She dropped them with a frown. He had much to be blamed for. Next to the vasculum was the walnut post box and the tray of letters arrived for her father. On top was an envelope postmarked Hereford. It was a letter addressed to Catherine Pendine. So who could be writing to the governess?

'Harriet, there you are at last. I've been waiting for you. You haven't forgotten your piano practice, I hope?'

In a single swift movement, Harriet dropped the letter into the vasculum and closed the lid. She turned to face her governess.

'I should like to paint the primroses first,' she said. 'They fade so quickly.'

Catherine gave an impatient sigh but did not object.

'Very well. Take them up to the schoolroom.'

In her room, Harriet rang for Annie, her maid, to help her change out of her walking skirt. Hurriedly she took out the envelope from the vasculum before it should get damp, and slipped into her sewing box to study later. With the key safe around her neck, she returned to the schoolroom with the little bunch of primroses to find her paints.

How serene the governess looked, seated by the window, head bowed over a book of poetry. Was she thinking of Robert Meredith? Harriet smiled as she thought of the letter from Hereford. She was impatient to return to her room and read it in private. She had to find out more about her governess. Perhaps the letter was the key to a secret past.

Impatiently Harriet retired to the drawing room after dinner, willing the governess to leave her. As Catherine bent over her poetry, Harriet opened her sewing box, threaded her needle with a length of silk, her hands trembling as she thought of the letter hidden at the bottom of the box. She worked swiftly, outlining the five heart-shaped petals of a primrose on a square of cotton. She would always remember that morning, and Robert Meredith, whenever she looked at the primrose.

Primroses for young love, she remembered from the language of flowers. *'I can't live without you'.* Was that how Catherine Pendine felt about him?

She embroidered the next piece of pale patterned cotton with a fern outlined in chain stitch. Ferns for sincerity. She thought about the letter. If she cut it open, she would then have no choice but to destroy it. It would be impossible to conceal what she had done. And yet, perhaps there was a way. Hadn't Cook shown her how to soak stamps from envelopes so that she could add them to her scrapbook?

Unable to contain her impatience any longer, she informed her governess she felt tired and had a slight headache, and rang for the maid. She fidgeted while Annie dressed her for bed and brushed her hair, complained that the jug of water was not hot enough, and waved her away.

'Leave the jug,' she told her. With her door safely closed at last, she took out the letter from its hiding place. Carefully she tipped a little of the hot water into the basin and floated the letter on top. Then she waited, like a cat at a mousehole.

'My dearest Caro, I am pleased you have found an agreeable situation,' the writer began. *'I am impatient to see you and cannot wait until that blessed day. May it come soon.'* It was signed with an initial only. A scrolling 'J'. So there was someone in Catherine Pendine's past, Harriet realised. A shock of triumph, and of hope, jolted through her. Someone who might yet come and take her away. Someone from Hereford. Belmont House. Hadn't Catherine's last employer been in Hereford? She had not spoken of her reason for leaving. *'My dearest Caro'* she murmured. It was intriguing. Had there been some scandal, perhaps? And what of Robert Meredith? Did he know he had a rival for Catherine's attentions?

She would have to visit Gwen, she decided, and show her the letter. She had to find out what had happened in Hereford. She held her cool hands against her flaming cheeks, her eyes feverishly bright. She was right after all. Catherine Pendine had a secret.

*

'Your father said you'll be seventeen next month. I thought, when he returns today, I should ask him if he

44

would hold a dinner party to celebrate your birthday,' the governess told her.

'A dinner party?' Harriet glanced up from the pages of her French primer. There had been no social gathering at Cropstone Hall since her mother's funeral. The thought of it alarmed her. She would have to play hostess. She shook her head. 'My father would never agree.'

'Why ever not? It will be a good opportunity for you to practise your skills as hostess. And you can play some of the songs you've learnt.'

'But who could we invite?'

'A few neighbours. Your aunt and cousins, of course. Why don't you draw up a list of guests this morning and I can discuss it with your father later.' Catherine said.

Harriet felt her face heat. 'Neighbours?' she said hoarsely. Did that include Robert Meredith, she wondered? After all, he meant to be acquainted with them sooner or later. She wondered what the governess's reaction would be if she added his name to the guest list.

'I'll need a new gown,' Harriet said.

'Of course you will. And since this will be the first of many social engagements, I'm sure your father will approve our visit to your dressmaker in Ludlow.'

Harriet smiled. Not at the prospect of new gowns. This would be a good opportunity to visit Gwen and show her the letter she had intercepted.

Her glance flicked over Catherine Pendine's plain gown. A governess was not provided with clothing as were the other servants, yet she must dress in a style appropriate to the family she worked for. Accompanying her charge to social engagements would always be a struggle on a small salary, and, Harriet

45

knew from Gwen, Catherine had little money of her own. Her clothes were plain and had already seen a great deal of wear.

'Do you have a gown for the party?' Harriet asked her.

Catherine gave a faint smile.

'I doubt anyone will notice what I'm wearing, Harriet.'

'A new lace collar at least?' she suggested.

'Perhaps,' Catherine said softly, her eyes downcast.

With her studies over for the morning, Harriet went to the library to fetch a volume on botany. She reached up from the wooden library steps and took down a leather bound volume from a high shelf. Clutching it, she passed the desk where she had left Robert Meredith's visiting card. It was no longer there. Had Mrs. Warren taken it? She left the book on the desk and hurried across the hall to the baize door that led to the kitchens.

Mrs. Warren, the housekeeper, was in her parlour, instructing the cook in readiness for Mr. Dash's return.

'Has my father's desk been tidied? I left something there for him and now I can't find it.'

'Lord, no,' Mrs. Warren insisted. 'You know how particular he is. No, Susan has been in to dust and polish, but she knows better than to touch the desk until he says so.'

'Then I must be mistaken.' She glanced at Mrs Marsh, their cook. 'We may be having people to dine with us in a few weeks. For my birthday,' she said.

'Yes, Miss Harriet,' the woman said warmly. 'Miss Pendine told us this morning.'

'Did she?' Since when was Caroline Pendine running the household? She turned her icy glance to the housekeeper. Mrs. Warren gave a nod of encouragement.

'Rest assured, I'm here to advise you, Miss Harriet. It's not just Miss Pendine who knows about dinner parties. You'll see.'

'Thank you, Mrs Warren. I'm most grateful,' she said.

The following Wednesday they travelled by train once again into Ludlow. Harriet, demure and obedient as ever, gazed out at the valley, the hawthorn hedges snowy with blossom, lambs tottering unsteadily behind the ewes in the meadow. In her bag she carried the letter from 'J'. She glanced at Catherine Pendine, certain the governess had taken the visiting card from her father's desk. Why was she trying to hide it? Because she wanted to keep her acquaintance with Robert Meredith secret? No matter. She could recite his address perfectly. She had it by heart.

'Robert Meredith Esquire, 5 Bell Lane, Ludlow.'

But what was in Miss Pendine's heart, she wondered?

Mrs Groves welcomed Harriet and the governess into her small salon of brocaded walls and silk upholstered chairs. She had been dressmaker to Harriet's mother for years, and looked fondly at the young woman she had known since childhood, and, with a quickened interest, at the new governess.

'Won't you sit down? The pattern books are here on the table for you to make your selection. A dinner party at Cropstone Hall is truly something to celebrate,' she said warmly. 'I'll have Megan bring us some tea.'

'If you'll excuse me, I have some errands to attend to,' Catherine said. 'I'll leave you in Mrs Groves' care,

Harriet. I'm sure her advice will be more valuable than mine,' she said lightly. 'I'll be no more than half an hour.'

Harriet stared at the pattern books, impatience brewing. She had to follow her. She had to find out where she was going.

'I'm so sorry, Mrs Groves, I'd quite forgotten,' she said the moment she heard the front door closing. 'I meant to ask Miss Pendine to find some music for me, for the dinner party.'

As she stepped down into the street, she caught sight of Catherine Pendine walking briskly down the hill away from the shops and the market place. Harriet followed at a little distance. As the governess turned the corner, Harriet glanced up at the street sign, and knew exactly where she was going.

She reached the corner and peered round. There, she could see her on the steps of a house. Moments later the governess was admitted. Harriet gave a dogged smile. It was just as she had suspected.

'Bell Lane,' she whispered. Why was the governess visiting Robert Meredith? And alone, and so furtively. And what of 'J'? Just who had Catherine Pendine set her heart on?

She retraced her steps, hurriedly retreating around the corner into Broad Street, afraid she might be seen from the window by Meredith or Catherine Pendine.

'Oh!' she gasped as someone barged into her.

'F-forgive me …!'

The young man stepped back, blushing scarlet, and swept off his hat.

'Oh … M-miss D-Dash … I'm so s-sorry …' He stared at her appalled, having himself been hurrying, head bowed, on an errand for his employer.

Her initially steely glare softened as she recognised him.

'Oh, please, don't apologise. I really should look where I'm going. I was in such a hurry myself. An appointment at the dressmakers,' she said with a warm smile. 'You're Lawyer Adcott's clerk, are you not?'

'Most kind of you to r-remember,' he said, taking comfort from her smile. 'S-Samuel Kendall.' He gave a stiff half-bow, reddening once more under her bright gaze. 'At your service.'

'*At your service*. Yes indeed. You may very well be,' she thought.

'I trust you are well, Miss Dash?' he asked, anxiously twisting his hat in his hands.

'Very well, thank you, Mr. Kendall.' Her eyes narrowed as she watched him. 'I mustn't delay you. You must be on important legal business. I wonder … is Mr. Adcott expecting Miss Pendine today? I believe she spoke of a meeting.'

'No, no. That matter's all concluded,' he assured her.

'Ah. I'm so glad. Only, I saw a letter come for her, from Hereford, you see. I was anxious that all was not well.'

The young man frowned.

'Mr. Adcott didn't mention meeting with Miss Pendine again. The papers were signed and witnessed, as I recall.'

'Then please don't trouble yourself about it,' she said breezily. 'Best if we forget about it completely. Good day, Mr. Kendall.'

'Good day, Miss D-Dash.'

Papers. Signed and sealed. Whatever could they relate to, Harriet wondered? As she turned the next corner, she found herself outside her aunt's house. The maid informed her that, regrettably, Mrs. Lindley was from home. Harriet, somewhat relieved, enquired after Gwen. It was evident from the distant squeals and cries that the children were very much at home.

'Miss Harriet, it's good to see you again,' Gwen said as she came hurrying down from the nursery to greet her. She looked flustered, pink-cheeked, strands of hair escaping from beneath her cap. Harriet surveyed her with a tender smile. How glad Gwen would be when she knew the governess had gone and she could return to her old life at Cropstone Hall.

'I'm in Ludlow to be fitted for a new gown. For my birthday party,' she told her. 'At least, we hope Papa will agree. Please tell my aunt she may expect an invitation very soon.'

'A party. Now there's a fine thing. And not before time, if you ask me.'

'There is some other matter I wanted to ask you about.' She produced the envelope from her bag and showed it to Gwen. As she took it, she gave Harriet a troubled look.

'But this is addressed to Miss Pendine.'

'Of course it is,' Harriet snapped. 'That's why I wanted your advice. I suspect Miss Pendine has a secret admirer. She is not all she pretends. This may give us a clue to her past.'

With a shake of her head, Gwen thrust the letter back at her.

'It isn't right, Miss Harriet. You must tell her at once what you've done, and apologise. No good will come of it else, you mark my words.'

'But Gwen, don't you see? Here is someone writing to her, begging to see her again. His initial is 'J'. Her last post was with a family in Hereford. She must have had a liaison of some sort there. Perhaps she broke his heart. Perhaps she has fled here from some scandal.'

'I'm sure Mr. Adcott will have evidence of her good character, Miss Harriet. You must put this behind you. It can only harm your own good nature, like a poison.'

Harriet gave a sigh. So Gwen was fooled by the governess's prim exterior, just as Adcott had been. No matter. She would seek the truth alone. Lightly she put her arm about Gwen's shoulders and hugged her, glad now she had not confided in her about meeting Robert Meredith, about the missing visiting card, and Catherine's visit to him. That could wait until she had proof of Catherine Pendine's duplicity. But one day, everyone would know the truth.

'I'm so glad to see you settled here,' she said as she took her leave.

'And that letter ... you'll take it straight to Miss Pendine and apologise?'

'As soon as I am able,' Harriet promised. Though that, she reasoned, would not be for some time.

'Harriet, I was beginning to worry ...'

Harriet saw the governess standing with Mrs Groves on the steps of the dressmaker's shop, looking anxiously up and down the street.

'I remembered just after you left, I wanted to ask you to find some music for me,' Harriet told her serenely. 'But when I reached the Square I couldn't find you.'

'No?' Catherine drew a calming breath. Her glance flickered to Mrs Groves. 'I told you I had some errands. Birthdays are meant for surprises.'

'Indeed they are,' Harriet said with a bright smile. 'I called on Aunt Isobel to tell her about the party and to expect an invitation, but she wasn't at home. I saw Gwen. She wanted to know everything that's been happening at the Hall since she left.'

There was no reason for Miss Pendine to doubt her. And, it seemed, she had not been seen by them from the house in Bell Lane. Her secret, at least, was safe. Which is more than could be said for Miss Pendine's, Harriet thought.

She sat beside the governess on the silk upholstered sofa in the dressmaker's salon, and studied the pages of designs. The slender waist and draped skirts that Catherine Pendine found so delightful blurred before her. All she could think of was Robert Meredith, and Catherine Pendine alone with him. Just how well did they know one another? Was Catherine in love with him?

With the pale pink silks and lace trim selected, Harriet followed Mrs Groves upstairs to the fitting room to be measured for her gown. The governess sat on one of the spindly gilt chairs beside the cheval glass, chatting amiably enough with Mrs Groves as Harriet stood rigidly to be measured. As she loosened her skirt and bodice, her stomach clenched. Around her neck hung the ribbon bearing the key to her sewing box. She watched Catherine's reflection, saw the moment Catherine noticed the key. Their eyes met. Harriet was aware of the thud of her heartbeat. Would she guess what the key kept hidden? Harriet's gaze steeled. Just how would her father react if he knew of the governess's secret visit to Robert Meredith, and of that letter, '*My dearest Caro*'. Yet it was Harriet's glance that dipped away first. There would be time enough for challenge later, when she was sure of the truth. And now, with the prospect of a return visit to Mrs Groves within a week, she had every hope that Samuel Kendall would indeed prove himself to be of service to her in her quest.

On their return to Cropstone Hall, Harriet went at once to her room to change her gown. In the few moments before her maid arrived, she hurried to her sewing box, unlocked it and returned Catherine Pendine's letter to its hiding place together with her diary.

William Dash, as had become his custom, summoned the governess to the library directly after dinner to inform him of Harriet's progress with her studies, and her plans for future lessons.

'Your father was pleased to hear of your progress at the piano,' Catherine informed her when she returned to the drawing room. 'And of course with your French verbs,' she added with a prim smile. Her eyes were distinctly cool, Harriet thought. Her glance went again to her neck, as if seeking the key.

The sewing box stood open on the little marquetry table at her side. Catherine sat down, hands clasped in her lap, and watched Harriet as she stitched her patchwork pieces. On one she had carefully embroidered the outline of a daffodil, symbol of deceit. On the other, the shape of a bell. Though she knew by heart the address she had concealed on the paper beneath it. Beside it she stitched a palm leaf shape. She was certain that the letter would secure her victory over the governess. Soon she would be rid of Catherine Pendine.

'Dear Papa. I hope I don't disappoint him,' Harriet said.

'I'm sure you won't. But we must work hard together,' she said. 'There must be no distractions.'

'Distractions?'

Catherine's hands tightened in her lap.

'I spoke to your father … about your botany studies. He has asked that you do not go out plant hunting alone, Harriet. We have far too much to do here, together, if you truly wish to please your father with your accomplishments.'

What was she afraid of, Harriet wondered? Did she know Meredith had come to the Hall and given Harriet his visiting card? Did she fear she would be blamed if Harriet met again with Robert Meredith while out walking? A gentleman of means must indeed be an attractive prospect to an impoverished governess. So she wanted Robert Meredith for herself. Poor 'J'. Evidently Catherine had fled from him because he was not as wealthy a prospect as Meredith.

'Of course,' Harriet answered softly. She saw the relief in the woman's face, the fingers relaxing. She saw the quick glance Catherine gave to the sewing box. Harriet smiled, secure in the knowledge that Catherine would not find the letter. Nor her diary. Indeed, since the previous evening, the pages of both had been neatly cut into hexagons and one by one stitched into the fabric of her patchwork, out of sight.

3

BRON

'*Need to do more research,*' Cat's note had said. As I drove out of Ludlow, I wondered if she had gone to Cropstone Hall. I checked the map. It was only a few miles across country from Bishops Castle, a short detour on my way home.

I turned off the main road at Horderley and made my way up the steepening bank of the valley. Through the trees I saw the glimmer of water, a wide stretch of lake. As I reached the high wrought iron gates, I pulled up. I could see the house now: its tall windows and porticoed front door had that distinctive Georgian elegance. The house was set like a jewel in a sweep of parkland, its pale stone offset by the darker backdrop of the wooded hillside where, according to the map, an ancient ridgeway track led through the trees. But if Cat had come here, how had she travelled? Was there a bus? Had someone given her a lift? Even if she had made her way here, where was she now? Somehow I didn't think I'd be welcome, turning up on their doorstep demanding to know if they'd seen a sixteen year old Goth.

More than likely she was waiting for me back at my cottage. I checked my phone. No messages. I started the engine, turned in through gates, and headed up the drive towards the Hall.

I waited anxiously on the wide stone steps of Cropstone Hall, admiring the view across the parkland to the lake, and wondering what the hell I was going to say if anyone was at home. Cat could be anywhere. Shopping. Meeting friends. *'Research'* she had said, and what was Cropstone Hall if not research?

There was no answer to my knock. I was glad. I could escape without having to explain what I was doing there. Then I saw a man come round the corner of the building.

'Looking for me?'

He was broad-shouldered, wearing a checked shirt and cord trousers with muddy green wellies. His dark hair was ruffled and he had that distinct glow to his face of someone who enjoyed an outdoor life. Yes, I could definitely be looking for him, I thought, ensnared by his assessing gaze and that disarming smile.

'I'm Bronwen Jones,' I got out, feeling hot in the sun's glare. 'I'm a textile artist. From Bishops Castle.'

He wiped his hands on his handkerchief.

'Grooming,' he said. 'Horses. I'm Gabriel Haywood.' He thrust out his hand at me. I took it, conscious of his strength, of his warm skin. Close to, he was older than I'd first judged. Around fifty, perhaps. There were strands of grey in his hair, and fine wrinkles radiated from the corners of his eyes.

'I've been given an antique quilt,' I plunged on. 'It was made by someone who used to live here in the 1880s.'

'Not guilty,' he said. 'I never mastered cross stitch. And I've only been here five years.'

'No. Of course.' I smiled, feeling stupid under his gaze, and cleared my throat, conscious it was now or never to ask about Cat. 'Has anyone been here asking about the history of the house today?'

He shook his head. 'Why don't you try the local library? I'm sure they'll have lots of stuff about the house and its previous occupants.'

'Yes, they did give me a potted history. The house belonged to the Dash family. It was one of the daughters who made the quilt. I wondered if you might have something dating back... old photos, maybe?'

'Sorry. The house has had a pretty major renovation. Don't think there are any skeletons left undiscovered,' he said.

'That's a pity. Well, not about the skeletons, obviously,' I said, flustered. 'Sorry to have troubled you, Mr. Haywood.'

'No trouble at all,' he insisted, his eyes gleaming as he smiled.

As I turned to go, something caught my eye: a glint of light among the gravel. A sequin. My heartbeat quickened. Cat had been wearing a sequinned T-shirt. So had she been here, asking about her ancestors? Then why hadn't he said so?

One sequin. It didn't prove anything. If Cat had called there, it didn't mean Gabriel Haywood had seen her. Probably out with his horses, I reasoned as I drove back through the pretty village of Edgton, towards Bishops Castle.

It was past four o'clock by the time I reached the cottage. There was no sign of Cat. I unpacked my carrier bags and trudged back down the lane to the next cottage to drop off Vi's shopping: a potent Stinking Bishop cheese, some smoked trout, and an armful of vegetables. Violet Bramley (*'like the tree, dear,'* she'd trilled at our first meeting) had lived in Apple Tree Cottage since she'd retired from a Ludlow accountancy firm ten years ago. I doubt she'd bought any new clothes since. A bit like Miss Haversham, she lived in the same kaftans, cheesecloth blouses and peasant skirts she'd had since the sixties. Perhaps her heart had been broken then. Certainly she never spoke of anyone else close to her except her sister in Bewdley.

I could hear '*Countdown*' blaring from the TV as I opened the back door. At least Vi would have a pot of tea made and, hopefully, some cakes. I piled her shopping on the table. There was a scuff of claws tap-dancing over the tiles as Vi's rakish Jack Russell came scurrying to greet me. '*Oh he's just William,*' Vi had introduced him. '*He's a bit of a rascal*'. Just William suited him. Luckily so far Vi bore no similarity to her namesake, Violet Elizabeth. At least, I hadn't yet heard her 'thcream'.

Vi flicked the TV to mute.

'Pistachio,' she said.

'Biscuits?' I asked hopefully.

'Anagram,' she said. 'But there's apple and sultana cake. Help yourself.' My favourite words. I did. It was still warm from the oven. Heavenly.

'I thought Clive was buying you lunch?'

'He did. It was a bit of a rush,' I said through sugary crumbs. 'The quiche was very good though. Salmon and watercress.'

The dog curled up on the sofa beside Vi and kept a watchful eye on the crumbs' progress.

'Vi, did you see anyone leaving my cottage early this morning?'

'No. What was he like?' she said, her eyes gleaming.

'She,' I corrected. I told her about Cat and the quilt, and her early departure.

Vi shook her head.

'If there'd been a car going past, William would have noticed.'

I told her about Nicky Price, the girl in the market, and what she'd told me about Ben Thomas's suicide a

58

year ago. And, less willingly, about my encounter at Cropstone Hall.

'Gabriel,' Vi said gleefully. 'Very Thomas Hardy.'

'But I'm definitely no Bathsheba. Besides, he's got probably got a wife and a string of thoroughbred children.'

'I went to a garden party there once. Vol-au-vents by the lake and a rather wheezy string quartet. Before his time, of course.'

'He didn't look the vol-au-vent type,' I conceded, though I wasn't entirely sure what 'type' I thought he was. That smile was disconcerting. Was Gabriel truly an angel? Or did he have a darker side? What if Cat were still there, locked up in one of those attic rooms? Was he more of a Mr Rochester? A house like that would have cellars too. A whole labyrinth of them. 'I just wish I knew where Cat is. That she's OK. Today of all days,' I said.

'I shouldn't worry,' Vi said briskly. 'She'll turn up when she needs feeding. They always do.'

But she didn't. Even though I'd made dinner enough for us both, and set an extra place at the table. I stood at the window of my studio and unfolded the quilt. I unpicked more pattern pieces and laid them out on the desk to decipher the writing, but I kept thinking about Cat, wondering where she'd got to. Why didn't she ring me?

After dinner, I switched on the computer again and glanced over the family tree Cat had started writing out. At least I could do some more research for her. I scrolled carefully through the 1881 census but nowhere could I find any trace of Catherine Pendine. I tried variations of her surname, substituted question marks for some of the letters, but still had no success. Where was she, that April? I searched for her in 1871, and found her in Hereford: aged 21, a governess, with two young girls in her charge. I tried the 1891 census, but again there was no trace of her. Probably she had married by then. I hoped so. There weren't many options for a woman of her age, other than teaching. At forty she would be considered too old as a companion for young ladies of marriageable age, and the rise of independent schools for girls had all but extinguished the need for finishing governesses. As I clicked to search the marriages index for her, there was a loud knock at the front door. It was almost ten o'clock. Cat. She'd turned up after all. As I hurried to answer the door, I decided I'd have to lay down some ground rules about timekeeping and letting me know where she was going.

'Where is she? You got her here?' the man demanded. He was shaven-headed, his face round and scarlet. His eyes seemed to bulge from their sockets in his fury. And, from his breath, I could smell he had been drinking.

I took a pace back, about to slam the door shut.

'Who?' I said, though I guessed exactly who he was looking for. I remembered the bruises on Cat's wrists. And now I had a pretty good idea who'd caused them.

'As if you didn't know!' His head jutted towards me. 'I'm Lee Brooks, Caitlin's stepdad. I've come to fetch her.' He barged past me into the narrow hall. 'So where is she? And don't you try denying it, neither. Her mate told me about you. What do you want with our Cat? Lesbo, are you? Cat!' he shouted.

'Obviously she isn't here,' I said as coldly as I could, and tried not to let him see I was shaking. 'And if you thought about it for a second, you'd realise that was why I was asking Nicky about her. I didn't know where she'd gone. I was worried about her.'

He reached the empty kitchen and glared back at me. 'Ran away from you, did she?' he sneered. 'See you for what you are? I should get the police for your sort!' he said, jabbing his forefinger into my shoulder.

'I'm sure they'd be interested to know about the bruises on her arms,' I countered.

'Bruises? What d'you mean?'

'I think you know exactly what I mean.' I held his glare, refusing to back away. His arms beneath the white vest were well muscled, and daubed with tattoos. I wanted him out of my house but I knew I wasn't strong enough to push him back and slam the door on him. Just how the hell was I going to get rid of him?

'What's she been telling you, the lying little bitch?' he demanded.

'She didn't have to say anything. I saw the bruises for myself. And unless you want to explain to the police exactly what happened, I suggest you leave now.'

'Oh, I'm not going anywhere. Not until I find out what's happened to Caitlin,' he said.

'She told me she'd left home. She wants to go travelling. I tried to persuade her to stay and finish her exams.'

'You a teacher or something?'

'No. I'm a textile artist.'

He frowned. 'Then why the hell did you want her staying with you?'

'She came here to ask me about a quilt. She wanted to know how much it was worth.'

'That old thing!' His eyes narrowed as he thought it through. 'You mean it's worth something then?' There was a new glint in his eyes.

'No! At least, I don't know yet.'

'She gave you the quilt, didn't she?' he said in triumph. 'Well, you can hand it over right now. You've no right …'

'It's Cat's!' I insisted, standing my ground.

He gave a derisive snort. 'Caitlin had no right to it. It's her mum's, and she wants it back.'

'That's not what Cat told me.'

'I'll bet!' he sneered. He pushed me back against the wall and strode into my studio. 'Where is it then?'

He stood in the middle of the room, his eyes casting about. I could see his fingers flex, sensed the latent rage in him. Any minute now he'd start pulling the place to pieces. My quilts, the months of work: how vulnerable they all seemed.

'Get out of here!' I yelled at him.

He spun round. 'You don't give me orders!' He took a step towards me, then another. Watched as I backed away from him, his smile broadening. 'What's the matter? Cat got your tongue, eh?' He gave a soft laugh at his own joke. 'What else did you get from her, then? Make you hot, did she? Is that it? You a lezzie, are you? Is that why you wanted Caitlin staying here? Make me sick, your sort!'

'Get out,' I uttered. I bumped back against the kitchen worktop. With nowhere else to escape to, I could only glare at him as he closed against me.

'You know what your trouble is? You never had a proper man,' he said. 'I can soon fix that. Don't know what you've been missing.' He grabbed hold of me, pulling me closer. His mouth fastened against mine. Suddenly, with a cry that blasted beery fumes into my face, he let me go. His eyes bulged in shock.

'What the 'ell?'

I was aware of the low growl then, like an engine. Looking down, I saw William had sunk his teeth into

62

the man's ankle, and was not letting go.

'Bloody mutt!' he yelled in pain and fury, trying to shake the dog free. 'Get him off me, you fat bitch!'

'The police are on their way. I suggest you leave immediately.' Violet Bramley's small shrill voice cut across the kitchen.

'Another bloody lesbo!' he gasped. Vi clicked her fingers, William released his grip, licking his lips, his small eyes brilliant with malevolence. William's ancestors had been good ratters, and Lee Brooks was a very large rat. Brooks stumbled past us, down the hall to the front door, leaving a spattered trail of blood.

My legs gave way. I flopped onto the chair, breathless and shaking, I heard the rev of a motorbike engine.

'William heard the bike going past,' Vi said briskly. She switched on the kettle and found two mugs. 'He started barking. We thought we'd just take a little walk and make sure everything was all right.'

'Thank goodness you did,' I said, my teeth still chattering.

'Horrible man, wasn't he, William? I hope he hasn't given you rabies.'

'He's Caitlin's stepdad,' I said.

'No wonder she was so eager to leave home.'

'But if she didn't go home, then where is she?' I said. 'Do you think I should tell the police?'

'About Caitlin? Yes. And about that horrid man? Definitely,' she said, with her severest look. 'William should've peed in his crash-hat.'

*

63

'She was at a talk about quilts I gave, on Monday night,' I explained to the young policewoman. 'She said her name was Caitlin. She turned up Tuesday afternoon with the quilt to show me. She said she'd left home and wanted to sell it so she could go travelling. I tried to talk her out of it. I told her she could stay here till she'd done her exams.'

PC Grace Cross glanced up from her pocketbook. She looked barely old enough to have left school. Slim, with curly dark hair, and an elfin face, she would not have looked out of place in an Arthur Rackham drawing.

'So Caitlin spent Tuesday night here?' she asked in her quiet calm voice.

I nodded. My hands clenched together in my lap. Surely she didn't think there was anything wrong with that? Had I been really stupid? I glanced down at William, curled asleep, in blissful unconcern, at Vi's feet. If he hadn't heard that motorbike ... I gave a shudder.

'Anyway, when she'd gone this morning, I didn't know what to do. I had a meeting in Ludlow, and saw a girl who looked like her. Turns out she was a friend of Caitlin's. I gave her my business card. She must have told Caitlin's step-dad and he turned up on my doorstep, sometime after ten, and threatened me,' I said, more calmly than I felt at the memory. I remembered his harsh voice yelling at me. '*Fat bitch.*' 'He'd been drinking,' I said. 'He yelled at me. He made ... accusations.'

PC Cross looked up at me, her glance steady, patient.

'What sort of accusations, Miss Jones?'

I glanced at Vi. She gave a stiff nod as if to say, *go on then, tell her what he said, tell her about the bruises.*

I told her. Though not about the '*fat bitch*' bit. She could probably see that for herself. She closed her notebook and got to her feet.

'Thank you for the tea and biscuits, Miss Jones.'

'Will you look for her? If she didn't go home, and she's not with friends …'

'Her mother has reported her missing. We're making enquiries. Thank you, Miss Jones. You've been a great help.'

'But hasn't her mother any idea where she is? Hasn't anyone seen her?'

'Caitlin's sixteen. It isn't that unusual in the circumstances. A family argument, pressure of exams,' she said gently. 'I'm sure she'll turn up safe and well. Sometimes they just need a little time to think things through. We'll check with her school and see if they were aware of any particular problems.' She glanced at her watch. It was almost two. 'I'm sure she'll be staying with a friend.' She gave me a reassuring smile. 'And if her stepfather threatens you again, call us straight away. The number's on my card,' she said. 'Don't worry. We'll have a word with him too.'

It was some time before I fell asleep, having checked and rechecked that all the doors were firmly locked and bolted, the windows shut even though the night was warm. Vi had even offered to loan William to me as guard dog for the night.

'He won't come back,' I said. I just wished I felt convinced it was true.

I woke around ten, with sunlight flooding in through the bedroom window. It was going to be a glorious day. I pulled on jeans and a baggy T-shirt, checked my phone, in a forlorn hope that Cat might have tried to get in touch.

Easing back the bolt on the French doors, I checked outside for any sign of movement, startled at the clatter of a pigeon taking flight. I cursed, and went about watering the newly planted pelargonium cuttings and salad leaves, and the tomato and pepper plants in the tiny greenhouse.

In the studio I spread out the silks and fabric stabiliser to cut yet more leaves for the wall hanging. On the table was Cat's quilt. I'd shown Vi the writing on the hexagons the night before while we waited for the police to arrive. She'd been as intrigued as I was. But as I folded it up and put it safely back on the shelf, I saw Cat's note again.

'Need to do more research.'

I knew it was hopeless trying to work when my mind was so distracted. The wall hanging would have to wait.

'Sorry Clive.'

I scooped up the embroidered leaves, the length of silk and instead carefully spread out the quilt Cat had left with me. Piece by piece I teased out more of the paper hexagons. On one fabric patch was the shape of a daffodil, in tiny chain stitch, its dark yellow heart filled with satin stitch. Enclosed within the fabric were two pattern pieces cut from a letter. I put them side by side.

'*Cannot wait until that blessed day. May it come soon*', I read. The fragment was signed with a 'J'. A love letter? And what '*blessed day*' did it refer to? A wedding day? Indeed, embroidered on the next piece was the outline of a bell. Surely that indicated wedding bells. But as I turned over the paper piece, I saw a name: Robert Meredith, and an address in Ludlow. Bell

Lane. So the bell was a symbol for an address. There was nothing random about the choice of embroidered shapes, I realised. They were all keys to the writing concealed beneath, as if Harriet had been anxious to remember where everything was hidden, like a treasure map. But what was the link between the daffodil and 'J'? I got up from the table and went to the bookshelves. Somewhere I knew I had a book on the language of flowers. I found the book on the top shelf with some of the plant books I'd kidnapped from Ed's collection. Flicking through, I found what I sought. The daffodil was a symbol of unrequited love. And of deceit. Was that it? Had Harriet Dash been betrayed by the man she loved?

On the next hexagon was an oak leaf shape, veined in featherstitch, just the way I had been sewing the leaves for the wall hangings. Oak leaves for bravery. Was that its meaning? I teased out the paper piece from the seams and turned it over. On the back was another name and address: Oakley, 16 Church Street, Hereford. Why was Harriet keeping these names secret?

I made a list of what I'd found, just as Cat had suggested. All the while as I worked, I sat tensed, waiting, listening for Cat's return. I went to make coffee and rummaged for a biscuit. I remembered the crumbs of mud her boots had left on the floor, the afternoon she had turned up. It had been dry for some days now. If she'd come up the lane from the bus stop, how come she'd got so muddy? I thought of the ridgeway track that led along the hill behind the cottage. Is that the way she had come, up from the valley, crossing the stream?

As I waited for the kettle to boil, I searched the online archive of the local newspaper. There it was, dated a year ago:

'Gifted student found hanged in popular beauty spot'. Ben had been a keen musician at Beechwood, an independent school near Ludlow. His body had been found by a fellow student in the woods below Bury Ditches, the iron-age hill fort just a few miles across country from my cottage. I could even see the trees from my studio window. The 'fellow student' who found him, I was certain, had been Cat. He had left a note saying, 'Sorry'. I sighed. Poor Cat. No wonder she hated trees. But what had driven him to such an extreme? Exam stress? Bullying? I glanced up involuntarily, locating the wooded slope where Ben had died. Cat must have seen that view too. Is that where she had gone? Had she made her way to Bury Ditches to pay tribute to her school friend on that grim anniversary?

Through Brockton, the lane meandered between a clutch of farms and barns before heading more determinedly up the steep hill to Bury Ditches. There were two other cars in the car park. As I got out of the Land Rover I caught sight of a blonde woman striding up the path, a black labrador trotting ahead of her.

The path climbed steadily between stands of foxgloves that fringed the conifer plantations. I reached the edge of the woods, out of breath, sweat staining my t-shirt, and swatted at the circling cloud of midges. The grassy mound of the hill fort loomed before me. The woman with the dog was nowhere to be seen. There was no sign of Cat either. I wondered just where Ben's body had been found.

I laboured on, climbing the steep bank of earth, onto the plateau at the heart of the ancient stronghold. In the centre was a stone cairn topped with a map etched with the names of the encircling hills: Caer

Caradoc, the Black Hills, Corndon, Stiperstones. The view was stunning; it felt like being at the heart of the world, and yet it was so peaceful, so remote. Only the houses of Bishops Castle were glimpsed through the trees, and to the east, a scattering of farms.

There was no sign of Cat. So what had I expected? I was wasting time. The police were looking for her. They knew what to do in cases like this. I had to trust them to do their job. And I needed to get on with mine. There was still so much to do if I was ever to be ready for the exhibition. Hot and tired, I trudged back down the slope. The sunlight through the trees shone golden on the new bracken fronds. I strayed off the path to pick some of the young ferns. They'd make a fine dye of pale yellow. It was then I saw it. Just off the track, on the border of the conifer plantation, was a tall beech tree, one of the few survivors of the old mixed woodland that had once colonised the hill slopes. Against the knotted grey-green roots lay a posy of wilted flowers, bound with a scrap of black lace: dog rose, elderflower, honeysuckle. Cat had left them there, I knew. She had come, as I had thought, to pay tribute to her friend. In loving memory.

Tears pricked at my eyes. A life destroyed so soon, and perhaps Cat was in danger too. I reached the car park and stared across the landscape of fields and distant hills. There was no bus service this far off the beaten track. How could she have got here? Someone must have given her a lift. Someone who knew where she was. A close friend. Someone she trusted. So why hadn't they told her parents or the police where she was?

At the cottage, I made a hasty lunch of bread and cheese, munching as I searched the internet again. I found the website for Beechwood School. The photos showed a grand country house, its parkland converted into playing fields and swimming pool. It boasted a reputation for excellence in art and music. There were pictures of beaming students clutching trophies, music ensembles, and a trailer for their end of year art exhibition. So this, I realised, was the school Cat attended too.

I found my map and spread it on the table. Bury Ditches was miles from Ludlow, difficult to reach without a car. And neither Cat nor Ben were old enough to drive. Beechwood took boarding pupils for weekdays and whole terms, but it also provided a daily school bus, collecting pupils from outlying farms and villages. Had Ben been a boarder there, or was Bury Ditches close to home for him?

In those Welsh borderlands, there were far too many Thomas families in the phone book for me to trek round them all, in the vague hope that they might know Caitlin. But another news item, from the time of the inquest, referred to him as a Henbatch student. Checking the map again, I found the valley of Henbatch was within reach of the Kerry ridgeway that ran close to my cottage.

I hauled myself up over the waymarked stile into the field, crossed into a beech wood, and clambering down the steep bank of a narrow valley where the scent of bluebells vied with the pungency of wild garlic. The track emerged at last into a buttercup-filled meadow bisected by the meander of a wider stream. The approach to the kissing gate and narrow bridge were muddy, trampled by cattle hooves. Is this the way Cat had walked last Tuesday? Across the wooden bridge I headed up the track. There was a cottage, hunkered down behind a stand of rowan and holly, and a ramshackle gate interlaced with netting. A hand-painted sign read 'End Cottage'. The small windows were dark, reclusive. I pushed tentatively at the gate. At once a dog indoors set up a raucous barking.

'Sorry … I was looking for Mrs. Thomas?' I called, aware there was someone peering out of the half-open front door.

'Down the valley,' a thin voice came back on the breeze. The door banged shut.

I retraced my steps, squinted at the map, and found another waymarked path. This time the house looked better cared for. Newly whitewashed walls under a crisp tiled roof. The small front garden was neat with clumps of lavender and sage bushes. Pots of geraniums gleamed beside the door. I knocked and waited. There was no car in view. No sound this time from indoors. Then, from the direction of the stream, I heard a loud splash and a child's shrill wail.

I ran on down the track and saw her sitting in the stream. Couldn't have been much more than five, I thought, with blonde pigtails, and baggy dungarees over a pink t-shirt. She was sitting bolt upright in the cold bubbling water, her face screwed up in shock.

'You're OK. I'm coming,' I said. I slithered down the steep bank, stepped into the water, and scooped her up.

'There, you're all right now,' I said, and set her on her feet again on the track. She sniffed back her tears, gave me a glare, and walked off stiff-legged in her wet clothes. Seconds later she broke into a scuffed trot and headed in at the gate further down the lane. I followed at a little distance, and heard a woman's voice, scolding.

'She was in the stream. She must have slipped down the bank,' I said as I reached the gate.

The woman bent and gathered the wet child into her arms, glaring at me in much the same way the girl had done.

'I just wanted to make sure she was all right,' I said.

'Thanks.' The woman's mouth was tight, unsmiling. She looked to be in her forties, hair long, ragged, about her shoulders, and wearing a man's shirt over jeans.

'Mrs Thomas, is it?' I said as she made to turn and go indoors.

'What do you want with her?' she snapped.

'Actually, it was Caitlin I was looking for. I hoped you might know where she was.'

I watched as she set the child down and shoo her indoors. Then she straightened and returned her attention to me, her arms folded, her dark eyes narrowed.

'What do you want with Caitlin?'

I took a deep breath. So I was right. This was Ben Thomas's mother. And she knew Caitlin. Well enough to shelter her?

'I'm a friend,' I said.

Again that hostile glare. 'You from the papers?'

'No. I'm a textile artist. I make quilts,' I said. I glanced past the pile of bulging rubbish bags and cracked terracotta pots of withered plants. Across the long grass two honey coloured hens scratched and pecked. A tabby cat watched thoughtfully from the top of a battered old shed. There were nettle clumps in the corner, and a rusted mountain bike caked with mud. Had it been Ben's? 'Cat came to me, Tuesday afternoon, with a quilt of hers,' I explained. 'She said she wanted to sell it. She stayed over, then next morning she'd gone. I don't know where she is. I just wanted to be sure she was OK.'

She nodded, and with a sigh, relented.

'She told me about the quilt,' she said. 'You'd better come in.'

'It's decaff. That OK for you?' she said, placing a mug in front of me on the kitchen table. The room was cool despite the heat outdoors. The small window let in little light, its square panes hung with a patchwork of coloured glass. There was no sign of the little girl, though I could hear footsteps pattering overhead.

'It was your son, wasn't it? Cat's friend ...' I said as gently as I could. She had turned away from me, but I saw her nod.

'A year ago. Doesn't get any easier,' she said.

She sank down onto the chair opposite me, frowning as she peered down into her mug as if trying to read the runes. 'Never thought he'd do something like that.'

'He was a musician?'

She nodded. 'Piano. I teach piano. Taught him since he was Izzy's age. He had a real gift for music. I wasn't sure ... about Beechwood, I mean. But it seemed such a great opportunity for him. A scholarship. Then who knows.' She hugged her arms about herself. 'Now I wish I'd kept him here. He was home-schooled, you see, till he was almost fourteen. Never did mix easily with other children ... He said music made him feel alive, he could communicate with his playing. But in the end ... it just got too much. I didn't put any pressure on him,' she said sharply, as if countering an accusation.

'He and Cat were close friends?'

She nodded, her gaze distant. 'She was often here, weekends. He'd work on his compositions. She'd sit curled up on the sofa, reading or drawing. Comfortable together, they were. Knew each other's secrets. Or so we thought.'

'His death must have been a shock for her too. She hadn't known how he was really feeling?'

'Perhaps it was all in the music, after all,' she said.

'I'm so sorry,' I said, though I knew words were inadequate. Nothing was going to make up for the son she had lost. But there was still Cat to keep safe. Now I was all the more concerned for how she must be feeling. Did she feel guilty at somehow letting Ben down, not knowing, not being able to save him?

'Was Cat here Tuesday morning?'

She gave a sigh. 'She brought the quilt,' she said, though with reluctance, as if she were betraying a confidence, as if she didn't entirely trust me. Couldn't blame her really, could I? 'She told me she was on her way to see you. She asked me if I thought she was doing the right thing.'

'About the quilt?'

'About leaving home,' she said. Her gaze rose to meet mine. 'I told her to go back. Do her exams and see what happened.'

'You saw the bruises on her wrists?'

'It wasn't the first time,' she said. 'They were always arguing. The usual teenage stuff. What she wore, who she was with, the music she liked … She still comes here, when it gets too much. A safe haven, I suppose. I don't mind. Glad of the company.'

'But … why doesn't she report him?'

'Him?'

'Her stepdad,' I said, but as I spoke, I saw her frown. And I remembered Lee Brooks' look of surprise when I'd challenged him about the bruises. '*What's she been telling you, the lying little bitch?*' he had demanded. So it was her mother she had fought with. The one person you rely on to take care of you, to protect you. No wonder Cat wanted to leave home.

'So where else could she have gone? Is there someone else she's close to?'

She shook her head. She half turned in her chair as Izzy came downstairs in a clean dress, a string of beads to her knees, and a smear of lipstick.

'There, all dry now?'

Izzy nodded solemnly and stalked past us into the next room. There was a scrape of furniture, then the steady climb and descent of piano scales.

The woman tensed, listening.

'She's only started playing since Ben …,' she said. 'She misses him dreadfully.'

'You've no other children?'

She shook her head.

'There's just the two of us now,' she said.

'Your husband …?'

'Couldn't hack it. Took off after Ben died,' she cut in. 'Good riddance.' She got to her feet, gathering up the mugs, and clattered them into the sink.

'It must be lonely for you,' I said.

'We manage,' she said sharply, her shoulders stiffened.

I could understand her not wishing to talk to me about what had happened to her son. I had no business prying into her life, into her relationship with Caitlin. But reticence was one thing. The edgy look, the tension that seemed to vibrate through her, was something different. I was sure she was hiding something. What was it she felt guilty about?

She dried her hands and foraged through the pile of papers, bills, sheet music, on the table, and held out some sheets of paper.

'Here, these are Caitlin's,' she said. I saw sketches of cartoon figures in bold black felt pen. A Barbarella-style woman, and gaunt cityscapes of towering buildings and spiked rails, gorilla-like creatures armed with what looked like machine guns and draped with ammunition belts.

'Cat drew these?'

She nodded. 'Not my thing, but she has a distinctive style. Manga, she calls it. She was hoping she could sell some when she got to London.'

'You think that's where she's gone? She said something about finding her Dad.'

'She'll be lucky,' she snapped. She went to the door and looked in at Izzy who was still doggedly pounding out her scales. She glanced back at me. 'Sorry, but I've got a pupil coming in ten minutes. I have to get ready.'

Back at the cottage, I spread out the map on the kitchen table and traced with my fingertip a line connecting the four of us: Henbatch, Bury Ditches, Cropstone Hall, and my cottage. On foot across the fields, Henbatch to Bury Ditches. It was possible. But Cropstone was some miles away. Cat had to have caught a bus or got a lift from someone. Whichever it had been, someone must have seen her on her journey to the Hall. Someone knew where she had gone. She couldn't just have disappeared. Had she caught a bus into Ludlow, then the train to London? She had no money. Not unless someone was helping her. I just hoped the police had managed to find some trace of her by now. I tried PC Cross's number and left a message. There was no more

I could do. Impatient and anxious, I hoped my quilting would restore at least some sense of calm.

But when I went back into my studio it was Cat's quilt I returned to. I felt the enigmatic patterns of leaves and flowers were trying to convey their story to me. I had all the paper pieces gathered together, but still was no nearer uncovering the secret Harriet Dash had so carefully stitched away. As I glanced around the shelves of boxes, I saw the lid on one of the shoeboxes that held fabric scraps and trimmings was slightly raised. As if someone had been there, looking for something. And as I took the box down and took off the lid, I knew where the scrap of black lace had come from, that Cat had fastened round wild flower bouquet for Ben. She had intended going to Bury Ditches that morning. And Cropstone, for her research. I knew she had been there, the sequin told me as much, but how?

The phone rang. I pounced on it, desperately hoping it would be news about Cat. But it was Clive.

'I've been trying to get you all morning,' he complained. My glance went guiltily to the unfinished wall hanging.

'I was busy working,' I said.

'Glad to hear it.' He sounded relieved. Which made me feel all the more guilty. 'I'm sending a photographer round. We need some shots for the catalogue,' he said.

'OK,' I said cautiously. 'When's he coming?'

'About six. That OK for you?'

I stared in panic at the pile of fabric as yet unsewn. Two hours? I'd never be ready. Two months would be a hard push as it was.

'I have to get the posters and catalogues printed. You haven't forgotten the exhibition's just six weeks away?'

'No. I'll be ready. I won't let you down,' I assured him.

'I'm relying on you, Bron.'

'I know. And I'm really grateful for the chance of a show,' I said, repentant. 'It's just that …' I took a breath. 'There's been a bit of a distraction,' I said. 'There was someone here, a girl. She brought me a quilt to look at. A family heirloom. She was trying to sell it. Anyway, she's gone. Disappeared, actually.'

'What do you mean, "disappeared"?' he said sharply.

'It's OK, I think she's probably on her way to London but … well, she'd had a row with her mum and left home. I let her stay here Tuesday night. Then yesterday morning, she'd gone. Just a note to say she was doing some research.' I told him, briefly, about my visit to Cropstone Hall, the Dash family home. 'I went to look for her. I just wanted to make sure she was all right.'

'And is she?'

'That's just it,' I said. 'I don't know. No-one knows where she's gone. But there's nothing more I can do. I've told the police, and that's that. Now I can get on with my work. No interruptions. Except for the photographer of course. Clive?' He was very quiet. I'd expected him to rant at me for wasting my time. I could just hear him breathing. Then a slight groan. He cleared his throat.

'I think,' he said, his voice oddly strained. 'I've done something stupid.'

'I didn't know she was a runaway, did I?' Clive said, pacing the length of the studio and back. 'She didn't tell me that.' His usually sleek hair was ruffled, his collar awry. His blue eyes turned to me, imploring. 'You know me, Bron. I'd never hurt anyone.'

'What happened exactly?' I demanded, panic growing with every second as I watched him.

'I'd been away for the evening, staying with an artist friend of mine. Lovely girl. I left around nine. It was a glorious morning. Bright sunlight, birdsong, hood down on the car, and everything flowering and blooming, Mozart's "*Soave sia il vento*" on the stereo.' He sighed. 'And then I saw her. A pretty girl. I could see that, even beneath the makeup. So I stopped the car.'

'Where, Clive? Where was she exactly?'

'Edgton. At the crossroads. She was at the bus stop looking at the timetable. I asked her where she was going and offered her a lift.'

'Where to?'

He sighed again. 'That's the thing, you see.' Anguish burned in his eyes as he leaned across the table and reached for my hand. 'Just a lift, you understand that, Bron, don't you? I wanted nothing from her.'

'Where, Clive?' I repeated.

'I didn't touch her. I wouldn't. She was far too young ...' He glanced at me, saw my glare. 'Bury Ditches,' he said. 'She said she wanted to go up to Bury Ditches.'

I considered the information, his protestations of innocence. Clive had always had an eye for a pretty girl, but I had no reason to suppose he had demanded anything from her in return for a lift. Clive just wasn't that type. All the same, I had to know exactly what had happened, what she had said. And, more importantly, where she had gone next.

'What time did you get to Bury Ditches?'

'Nine thirty, maybe a quarter to ten. I was in no rush. Irena was there to open the gallery, and I wasn't due to meet you in Ludlow till twelve.'

Caitlin had already been to Cropstone Hall by nine thirty, so she must have a lift from my cottage, or else caught an early bus. But when Clive had left her at Bury Ditches, just before ten, she was safe and well. So why didn't I feel reassured?

'She said she was meeting someone,' he said, still pleading to be believed.

'Did she say who?'

'No. I didn't ask. Boyfriend, I assumed.'

'You didn't see anyone else there?'

He frowned, trying to remember.

'No. I'm sure I'd remember... No, the car park was empty.'

'So she just got out of the car, and that was it?'

'Of course it was,' he said crossly. 'I wasn't altogether happy at leaving her alone in such an isolated spot, but she seemed perfectly content. She smiled, gave me a peck on the cheek and that was the last I saw of her. I swear, Bron, nothing happened.'

He reached across the table, his hand tightening around mine. Just for a moment, I tensed. Was I wrong to trust him without question? I swallowed. Of course it was absurd to doubt Clive. He was used to leading a charmed and easy life. He would never risk losing that.

'It's OK,' I reassured him, enfolding his hand. 'But did she tell you why she wanted to go there, of all places, at that time of the morning?'

'She told me about the boy,' he said dully. 'Put rather a damper on the sunny atmosphere actually.'

'She didn't tell you why she'd gone to Cropstone Hall, did she? Or if she'd spoken to anyone there'

He shook his head. 'Didn't mention it. But she did tell me about her drawings. I'd told her I was an art dealer. When we stopped in the car park at Bury

Ditches, she pulled some drawings out of her bag. She asked me if I'd buy them. They were good, in their way. She has a distinctive style, but it's not my forté. I told her I had a friend in London.' For the first time since he'd arrived at the cottage he stopped fidgeting. He almost smiled. 'I gave her his number. Cartoons are his speciality. You said you thought she'd gone to London, didn't you?' he said more eagerly.

'I did. I just don't know for certain. Not unless someone saw her.'

He exhaled with a distinct relief.

'London. That's it, Bron. That's where she's headed.'

'When you left her ...'

'In the car park, safe and sound,' he said, holding up his hands, all innocent.

'Was she carrying any flowers with her?'

'Flowers? No. Why?'

'There was a bunch of wild flowers left at the place Ben died. I think she picked them as she walked up the path, that's all. She'd taken a scrap of lace with her from my stash here at the studio.'

'Stop worrying,' Clive said. 'She'll be in London by now, having a great time.'

'Let's hope you're right,' I said.

'I'll phone Andrew, that colleague of mine I mentioned. If she does turn up at his gallery, he'll let me know.' He frowned again, and looked anxiously at me. 'Bron, you will find her, won't you? Make sure she's all right. I can't live with this. Can you imagine the publicity if anything's happened to her ... if the police knew I was with her ... I can't do this. You understand that, don't you?' he implored. 'Now of all times. It would ruin me. The gallery. Everything.'

'Clive, stop panicking,' I said coldly. 'As you said, she's gone to London, OK?'

'But you're not sure.'

I drew in a deep breath. 'No. I'm not. But maybe if I can find out who she was meeting, and where she went after Bury Ditches, then I'll be closer to being sure she's OK. If it's London she's gone to, someone must have given her a lift. How else could she have got to the station?'

'Yes. That's it. Find out who she was meeting,' he said more eagerly. 'Discreetly though,' he said sternly. 'I mean, I can't risk being involved. If word got out … If anyone asks, I can't admit to having seen her.'

'The police, you mean?' I demanded, angered by his selfishness. What if Cat was truly in danger? If something had happened to her?

His look was answer enough. I let out a disdainful snort.

'Then you'd better just hope I find her safe and well.'

'The photographer … not a word to him, Bronwen. I'm trusting you,' he called back as he headed down the path to his Jaguar.

I slammed the door shut and stood, arms folded, until my anger cooled. I stalked back down the hall into the studio.

I pushed the lengths of dyed muslin and the quilt batting to one side. I was in no mood to start assembling the '*Autumn*' quilt.

Instead I spread out Cat's quilt and the notes we'd transcribed from the paper pattern pieces. An incomplete journal that somehow told a story from the initial rose and key motifs, to those final sprays of leaves and flowers. A bridal quilt? I had thought so. Yet there was no evidence I could find of Harriet Dash's marriage, nor indeed of what had happened to her governess, the mysterious Catherine Pendine.

I heard a car approaching up the lane. Clive said the photographer would be coming at six. He was early and I wasn't ready. I fled upstairs to brush my hair and put on a smear of lipstick, hoping it didn't have quite the same effect as Izzy's efforts. I raced back downstairs to answer his knock. But as I pulled open the door, I found it was a uniformed policeman standing on my doorstep.

'Bronwen Jones?'

'Yes?' I faltered. Something must be wrong. Had they found Cat? Had they been to question her stepdad? What if he'd complained about Vi's dog biting him? What if he'd come about Ed? That business in the car park? Surely it was too long ago now? All the same, I could feel my heartbeat racing.

'Miss Jones, I have a few more questions.' PC Talbot's blue eyes had a steady torchlight gaze. His square-jawed face was fair-skinned and slightly sunburnt, beneath cropped hair that was a ripe corn blond.

'What's happened?' I said, hoping I didn't look as guilty as he made me feel.

'Perhaps we could discuss this inside?'

'You told my colleague you'd seen a friend of Caitlin's in Ludlow yesterday,' he said, seated across the kitchen table from me. I hadn't offered coffee. 'A young woman who, you said, who looked a lot like her.'

'Yes. It was lunchtime. I saw her go past the window of the bistro. I thought it was Cat. Well, she was wearing a black T-shirt like Cat's. The one with the sequinned dragon. Why?'

'We're simply trying to establish the girl's movements,' he said. 'So, you approached Nicky Price in Ludlow market.'

'I told you. I thought she was Caitlin. She looked about the same age. I asked her if she knew Cat. I was worried about her. I didn't know where she'd gone. I gave her my business card so she could get in touch with me if she saw her.'

'Your business card.' He nodded, as if that was somehow the heart of the riddle he was trying to disentangle.

'Yes. That must be how Lee Brooks knew where to find me. Nicky must have given him my card.'

Again he nodded, and glanced down at his notebook again. Then the searching gaze returned to me. 'What time was it when you spoke to Nicky?'

'Why? It's Caitlin that's missing,' I said.

'Miss Jones, the body of a young woman was found earlier today. She's been identified as Nicola Price.'

'No,' I gasped. 'You're sure it's Nicky?'

'We're trying to piece together her movements yesterday. Who she saw, where she went.'

I felt sick. I got up and went to the sink to fill the kettle. Coffee. I just needed something. I felt dizzy, disoriented. Had Caitlin made it safely to London as I'd hoped? Again in my head I could hear Clive's voice. 'You know me, Bron. I wouldn't hurt anyone.'

I clutched to the sink edge: anything solid in this suddenly disintegrating world.

'Where? Where did they find her?'

'Bury Ditches,' he said.

'Dear Lord …' I whispered.

'Miss Jones?' Dimly I was aware of his concern.

'I … I was there. This morning,' I said. 'Looking for Caitlin.'

'What time was that?'

'Around eleven, I suppose.' I glanced back at him. 'I didn't see anyone. Well, not anyone like Nicky. Just a woman walking her dog.'

'I'd appreciate a description, Miss Jones, if you can remember. So you didn't see anyone else there? Any other cars?'

'I didn't take too much notice,' I said. 'I never thought for a minute… When did they find her?'

'Lunchtime. But she'd been there since the previous evening we think.'

'Where? Where exactly was she found?'

'In the bushes close to the car park. It seems her body had been dumped there,' he said. 'A woman found her. She'd been walking her dog.'

'How did she …?'

'She'd been strangled,' he told me, his voice flat, emotion carefully suppressed. I glared at him in horror. How could he sit there so calmly? Yet I knew he must have seen many such horrors before. His job, wasn't it? I shuddered. Only yesterday lunchtime I had seen Nicky, very much full of life. And now … I shuddered.

'That's awful. Have you any idea … who could have done it?' I asked.

'As I said, we're trying to trace who she saw, where she went, yesterday.'

I managed to fill two mugs with coffee and carried them back to the table, my hands shaking. I took a sip, burning my lips.

'You said you went to Bury Ditches looking for Caitlin?' he prompted.

I nodded. 'I was worried about her. I wanted to be sure she was safe,' I said weakly. I told him about her staying over Tuesday night, then disappearing yesterday morning. 'She left me a note.' I got to my feet and went into the studio to find Cat's note, and handed it to him.

'*Research*.' He glanced up at me, waiting for an explanation.

'Her family tree,' I said. Should I tell him about the sequin I'd seen on the gravel at Cropstone Hall? I knew Cat had been there, but it had nothing to do with what had happened to Nicky. One girl dead, another disappeared. No, there couldn't be a connection, could there? I glanced at him desperately. I had to tell him. He had to know about the sequin. Whether it meant anything, it was up to him to find out.

'A sequin?' he said, puzzled.

'The T-shirt Cat was wearing had sequins on it,' I said. 'I think she might have gone to the Hall because of the quilt. The one she brought to show me. It was made by her great-grandmother's grandmother, Harriet Dash. She lived at the Hall in the 1880s.'

'And you found a sequin?'

I nodded. 'On the gravel by the front step.'

'And this was when exactly?'

'On my way back from Ludlow. Yesterday afternoon.'

'And why did you go to Cropstone Hall?' he asked, his tone even, though somehow he seemed to be struggling to control his impatience and disapproval.

'Same reason as Cat. I wanted to find out more about the quilt,' I said. 'But when I met the Hall's owner, Mr. Haywood, he said he didn't know anything about the Hall's history. And he said no-one had been there asking about a quilt or the house or anything.'

'Cropstone Hall,' he repeated, jotting the name in his notebook.

'It was Nicky Price who told me about Ben Thomas,' I said. 'He was a friend of Cat's. That's where she found him hanged a year ago. It was the anniversary of his death. I saw she'd left some flowers there.'

'We noticed,' he said, again without emotion.

I took a breath. 'The strip of black lace, she took that from here. I keep a box of trimmings, scraps, all sorts really,' I said weakly. I could feel my cheeks heat as I thought of Clive's desperate plea, '*I can't risk being involved*, and his protestations of innocence. Yet Nicky was already dead, her body dumped out of sight by the time Clive got there with Caitlin. He couldn't be involved. I glanced anxiously at PC Talbot. 'Do you think Nicky's death has anything to do with Caitlin disappearing?'

'It's too early to say at this stage. Both enquiries are ongoing,' he said, closing his pocketbook. 'We're keeping an open mind.' His glance fixed on me again. 'Do you often invite strangers to stay overnight in your home, Miss Jones,' he asked. 'Young girls, particularly?'

I glared at him. So much for an 'open mind'. Had Lee Brooks been repeating his vile accusations to them?

'Of course not.'

'But Caitlin was different?'

'She was obviously in some distress. She said she'd left home and wanted to go travelling. She just needed a little time to sort things out.'

'You didn't think of ringing her mother and telling her where her daughter was? You didn't think she'd be worried?'

'Of course! I told Cat she could only stay if she contacted her mum. She texted her. I saw her do it.'

He nodded. 'But you didn't speak to her mother? Or see the number she'd sent the text to?'

I gave a sigh. 'No. I believed her,' I said, feeling stupid. From his look, he evidently agreed with me.

The clear blue eyes fixed on me again.

'How did she get here, Miss Jones?'

Again there was that quiet but strained patience in his tone. What was he expecting me to say? That I'd kidnapped the girl? Bundled her into the back of my Land Rover and driven her here? 'She walked,' I said. 'She'd been visiting someone locally. Ben Thomas's mother, actually.'

'And you invited her to stay here?'

'No. It wasn't like that. Not exactly,' I said desperately. I repeated what I'd told PC Cross, about my quilt lecture, and Cat turning up with the photo. 'She said she wanted to sell the quilt so she could go travelling. She wanted me to get a valuation for it, and to help her find out a bit more about her family history. We did some research online then I made up the sofa bed and left Cat to it.'

'Online,' he repeated. I stared at him. 'So you don't know if she made contact with anyone on the internet? Arranged to meet them?'

'No, ' I said, feeling all the more stupid. 'How could I? I was asleep.'

If I had been worried about Cat before, now I was beginning to see a whole new array of dangers. And, I realised, I was also beginning to think Lee Brooks had a point. I had no right to interfere in their lives. I could be the cause of putting her in harm's way. I stared at him, willing him to reassure me, to tell me that I hadn't messed up. Instead he just sighed.

'And yesterday morning … you say she'd gone when you woke up. Gone to Cropstone Hall. Any idea how she got there?'

'By bus, I think. I really don't know,' I said crossly. 'Sorry. I'm just worried about her, that's all. Especially now I know about Nicky.'

'We're all concerned, Miss Jones,' he assured her brusquely. He got to his feet. 'Let us know if you remember anything else, won't you? And of course if Caitlin gets in touch.'

'Yes of course. Thanks,' I said with a weak smile. 'I just hope you find something soon.'

'It would be useful to have one of our people check your computer. See if Caitlin had been using any internet chatrooms. I'll have someone contact you.'

I stared at him with a new fear. Had Caitlin contacted someone Tuesday evening while I was asleep? I couldn't bear to think of her walking into danger. But what if the danger were closer to home? I remembered the strength of Lee Brooks' arms as he'd grabbed me. Her fights with her mother were one thing, but I also knew her stepdad had a temper, especially when he'd been drinking. But that didn't mean he'd harm Cat. Or Nicky Price, for that matter. Did it?

'There is something else,' I said as he reached the door. I drew in a deep breath. Sorry Clive. There were some things that couldn't remain secret, even between friends. 'You asked me how Caitlin might have got to Cropstone Hall. I don't know, but I do know how she got from the Hall to Bury Ditches yesterday morning, to put flowers where Ben died. Someone gave her a lift.'

With a dull ache that was part foreboding, part resignation, I reached for the phone the moment the door closed.

*

89

'Sorry I'm late,' the young man said, his grin wide. 'I saw the police car leaving. At least they've not arrested you then, eh?' He swung his camera bag from his shoulder and made to come in.

My cheeks were still burning after my short, but succinct, conversation with Clive.

'I don't think you'll be needed,' I said. 'Clive's just cancelled the exhibition.'

'Hold on, hold on,' he said, staying the door as I made to close it. 'Clive never said nothing to me ...'

Just then, his mobile rang. And seconds later, as he clipped his phone shut, he gave me a pitying look.

'Well, you've really pissed him off,' he said.

'Oh my dear, I'm so sorry,' Vi said as she ushered me into the warm and softly cushioned comfort of her front room. She studied me with her bright robin-like gaze, head cocked to one side. 'After all your hard work too. But you did the right thing.'

'I hope so. Though I'm not sure it'll be so easy to find another gallery to take me on,' I said ruefully.

'It'll blow over,' she said. 'Talent like yours will out.'

'Like murder?' I suggested.

'Ah yes.' She looked sorrowful. 'To think of that poor girl, up there on the hillside. Dumped like a sack of rubbish. Hanging's too good for them.'

'You don't think Clive could possibly ... no, I don't believe it,' I said, shaking my head. 'Forget I said it.'

Vi studied me intently.

'You mean Caitlin might not be the only one he gave a lift to?'

'No. No, Clive just isn't like that. Besides, he was with a girlfriend Tuesday evening and didn't leave her till just before nine Wednesday morning. He couldn't have met up with Nicky.'

'OK. So he has an alibi. But who else might she have met?'

'That's for the police to sort out,' I said, but I was thinking of Lee Brooks. We both were. After all, he'd been in touch with Nicky and found out my address. Just how well did he know her?

'Tell me about the woman in Henbatch. Ben's mother,' she said. 'You said you thought she was hiding something.'

'She just seemed, well, edgy, I suppose.'

'Some people are like that. Not good in company. She must lead rather a secluded life.'

'She's a piano teacher. She's used to meeting people.'

'I suppose. Poor thing. This will all bring it back for her, of course.' Her look brightened. 'I'm sure she'd be glad of a little sympathy right now. Why don't you go back and see her?'

'I couldn't. She made it plain enough I wasn't really welcome there. And, no, before you suggest it, I'm not going to start learning the piano.'

'It was just a thought. So what about your dashing horseman, Gabriel whatsit? Do you think he could be a modern Bluebeard?'

'Hardly! He was perfectly charming.'

'So was Crippen, they say,' she muttered darkly. 'I'm just saying, if you want to find out where Caitlin went, you'll need to ask a few more questions, that's all. Caitlin had been to the Hall. You found the sequin.'

'Yes, but Gabriel Haywood said he hadn't seen her. Probably out riding. It was Clive who gave her a lift to Bury Ditches. And she told him she was meeting someone.'

91

'Ah yes, the mysterious 'someone'. A boyfriend, you reckon?'

'I just don't know. I can hardly ask her Mum.'

'So ... if Gabriel was out riding when she called, what if she went back there later that day?'

'Vi, no ... it can't have anything to do with him.'

'No?'

'He said he hadn't seen anyone there.'

'And of course you believed him,' she said sternly.

'I can't just waltz back in there and search the place for Cat.'

'No,' she said, thoughtful, reaching out to scratch the back of William's ears as the dog lay curled on a cushion beside her. 'You could always borrow William,' she said. 'Take him for a walk. But be careful. He does have a habit of running off.'

There was no way I was going back to Cropstone Hall, I decided. Even if I did see Gabriel Haywood again, I could hardly challenge him. He'd already told me he hadn't seen Caitlin at the house. I could hardly accuse him of lying. I switched on the computer and checked the recent searches. There were the usual family history websites and record offices. Then Facebook came up. Had Cat been in touch with someone the night she had stayed with me? Had she made plans to meet someone?

I yawned. It was getting late. There was nothing more I could do. I would just have to wait till the police had done their investigations, and hope, desperately, for the best. In the meantime there was another older mystery that was still intriguing me, and I doubted even PC Talbot could cluck with disapproval at my detective work in a mystery that was a hundred years old.

I made another coffee and set about searching for the Oakleys in Hereford. A name on a paper hexagon.

But what linked them to Harriet Dash, I wondered?

'Oakley! There you are,' I whispered as I scrolled down the census page for 1881. Mr and Mrs Oakley with one son, aged six, a daughter of eight, and an older daughter of seventeen. Harriet's age. Plus two domestic servants. One cook, one kitchen maid. No mention of a governess though. I scanned back to the 1871 census, where Catherine Pendine had been working for another family in Hereford, a governess in charge of two daughters of fifteen and sixteen. Had she known the Oakleys? Or were they to be Catherine's next employers? It looked as if Harriet had been doing some research of her own into her governess's background. But why? The answer had to be somewhere in that quilt.

4

HARRIET

It was as much as Harriet could do to stand still while Mrs Groves pinned up the hem of her new gown.

'You look a picture,' Mrs Groves assured her, standing back to admire her handiwork. 'Your dear Papa will be so proud of you.'

'Do excuse me. I have some invitations to deliver,' Harriet said, struggling out of the gown as swiftly as she could. The governess had already disappeared into the market place, leaving her in Mrs Groves' safe keeping.

Harriet hurried back up the street and paused on the steps of the lawyer's office to calm herself, her cheeks glowing at the thought of her mission.

'M-Miss Dash,' Samuel Kendall said, scrambling to his feet, his inky fingers hovering, anxious to take her hand yet overawed at the thought of touching her. 'Mr. Adcott is not in the office this morning.'

'No matter. I came to deliver his invitation to my party,' she said brightly. 'I hope I may entrust it to you.'

'B-by all means,' he answered, his face growing pinker by the minute.

Harriet fished in her bag and produced the envelope she sought. As she handed it across the desk, she contrived to drop a small white cotton glove on the floor, holding his glance with her smile. She took her leave as swiftly as she could, hurrying down the steps, across the street, and into the churchyard. Moments later she heard him come after her, calling her name.

'Not yet. Not yet,' she whispered, hurrying away between the gravestones.

94

She paused and turned at last with a look of alarm.

'Why, Mr. Kendall!' she said. 'Whatever is the matter?'

'F-forgive me, Miss Dash,' he said desperately, his jacket askew and missing his hat. 'Your g-glove,' he uttered, and held it out to her at a distance of some three paces.

'That's most kind of you,' she said, returning a pace towards him. He drew nearer, proffering the glove. Delicately she took it from him, and restored it to her hand, drawing the thin fabric over her fingers with infinite care, under his spellbound gaze. She gave a little shake of her head, sending her curls bobbing beneath the rim of her bonnet. 'My thoughts are in such a whirl, I can think of nothing else but my birthday party.'

'I'm happy to be of service,' he assured her, with a little bow, and reluctantly turned to go.

'Mr. Kendall, I wonder, could you be of further service to me? A small thing, but I wish it would be our secret.'

'Oh?' He returned to her, brightening. 'If I can help at all.' His eyes in his smooth round face glowed brightly with unabashed devotion.

'My governess, as you know, was last employed in a position in Hereford. I gather her pupil was most accomplished at the piano. I fear I'll never be her equal,' she confided. She saw him prepare to demur, but pressed hurriedly on. She had no use for flattery. 'I should so like to please her. Do you think I might write and ask them which piece of music was her favourite? I could play it at my party. It would be such a lovely surprise for her. What would you advise?'

'I … Well, I … I think it's a charming idea,' he assured her. 'I'm certain your playing will delight her.'

Harriet was less certain, but her smile was unwavering.

'Thank you, Mr. Kendall. You've quite put my mind at rest. I shall write to them at once.'

'My pleasure,' he told her with another low bow.

'I wonder … could you remind me of Miss Pendine's former address? I hate to be such a bother.'

'It's no trouble at all. I recall it exactly. She was with Mr and Mrs Oakley in Church Street, Hereford,' he said.

'Such a memory, Mr. Kendall,' she said in a show of awe. 'I'm in your debt.'

Harriet hurried back down the hill to deliver her aunt's invitation to their house in Raven Lane, and sought a few moments alone with her former nanny.

'Would you receive their reply on my behalf and send it on to me,' she told her as she hastily wrote out the address on the envelope she had brought with her. 'It must be a secret from Miss Pendine. I want to surprise her when I play her favourite piece for her.'

Gwen gave her a gentle hug.

'I'm so glad you've come to accept her, my dear. And I hope she wasn't too vexed about that letter of hers you took?'

'She said not a word about it,' Harriet assured her. Which, after all, was not exactly a lie, she reasoned.

She called at the post office on her way back to the dressmakers, and wondered impatiently what the response from the Oakleys would be.

'I am seeking information about a former governess who was in your employ. Catherine Pendine has applied for a position with us, and I should be grateful to receive your estimation of her character and her suitability as governess for my daughter.'

96

The letter was signed by a Mrs Gwen Lloyd.

That evening after dinner, Harriet worked at her embroidery, stitching the outline of an oak leaf in her tambour frame. She cut the piece into a hexagon and backed it with a scrap of paper bearing the Oakleys' address in Hereford. She overstitched it to the next hexagon, one she had embroidered with a hollyhock, a token of ambition: both hers and Catherine Pendine's. But only one of them would be successful.

With just two weeks until her birthday party, Harriet spent the morning practising her piano pieces and recitation. Catherine Pendine had been summoned to the library to report to William Dash on his daughter's progress.

'Miss Harriet, there's a letter come for you,' Annie said as Harriet finished playing. As she took the letter from the salver, she recognised Gwen's handwriting. Had she received a reply from the Oakleys in Hereford already? Her fingers trembled. She desperately wanted to open the letter at once, but was afraid her governess might return at any moment. She slipped the letter into the pocket of her skirt and made her way sedately, but with a pounding heart, into the hall.

The library door opened. For a moment Catherine did not see her there. As she softly, slowly closed the door, she gave a contemplative smile.

'I've finished the Mozart piece,' Harriet announced, pleased to see the governess look startled.

'Oh, yes … we could hear your playing. Your father was full of admiration at your progress,' she said.

'It's such a fine morning, I think I shall pick some flowers to paint. Will you come with me?' Harriet said. 'I shall only be in the Rose Walk.'

Catherine glanced back towards the library door.

'The Rose Walk? No further than that?'

'Of course. Aren't the flowers wonderful at this season?' she said sweetly.

Miss Pendine smiled in return.

'Enjoy your walk. I shall prepare some poetry for you to study this afternoon,' she said.

Harriet smiled, her hands brushing her skirt, aware with a sudden jolt of alarm of the slight rustle of paper from the envelope hidden in her pocket.

'I'll go and fetch my vasculum.'

Harriet paced briskly along the tiled path between the wide flowerbeds where Roberts, the gardener, and one of the boys were tying in the flowers to their supports, pruning back and deadheading the roses. Roberts paused to doff his hat to her, the young boy snatching off his cap.

She reached the summerhouse at last, and glanced back at the house. No sign of Catherine Pendine, and the gardener and his boy were too busy in the flower borders to pay her much heed. She tugged open the door and stepped into the musty stillness, her boots crunching over the dust and dry mud of the tiled floor. Cobwebs draped from the pitched ceiling, laced about the stacked furniture, in storage till the weather grew warm again. She dragged one of the wicker chairs to the window and sat down. With eager, shaking fingers, she drew the envelope from her pocket and tore it open, extracting a further envelope postmarked Hereford.

'Just as I thought,' she whispered as she hurriedly scanned the single sheet contained within.

'Miss Pendine was proving to be an excellent tutor, and my daughter was quite taken with her. It was regrettable that, due to her family circumstances, she

was obliged to resign her post with us. It was a cause of some inconvenience to us at the time. However, I would expect her to fulfil her duties diligently in any new position she may obtain.'

Family circumstances. Harriet clenched her fist about the sheet of paper. What exactly had happened in Hereford to force Catherine Pendine to leave her post so suddenly? If she had been involved in any scandal, Mrs Oakley would have told her. There could be no shadow of disgrace or shame attaching to so important a post. Then what? Had it to do with 'J' perhaps? A marriage proposal she had declined? And why? What had Robert Meredith to do with her? Was he the one she truly loved? Did he love her?

Harriet gave a sigh of frustration. How was she ever going to discover the truth and be rid of the governess? Who could tell her, other than the governess herself? Who, indeed?

With a sly smile, she thrust the letter back into her pocket and retrieved her sketchbook. Stepping outside again, brushing the dust from her skirt, she began to devise a new plan. Following the path through the garden, she found a spray of forget-me-nots growing in a gap between the tiles that had so far evaded Roberts' hoe. She stooped to pick them, tucking them for safety into the damp cloth inside the tin vasculum she carried strung over her shoulder, and returned indoors.

'Forget me not, indeed,' she thought. There were a great many memories she would need to stir up from the governess's past.

After dinner that evening, she embroidered a patchwork piece with the arching reflexed petals of a cyclamen flower. A cyclamen was a token of farewell, and she fervently prayed that soon, very soon, she would bid goodbye to Catherine Pendine. Carefully she cut two hexagons in paper, and stitched the fragments of Mrs Oakley's letter into the fabric, out of sight, beneath the forget-me-not pattern.

Her final fitting at the dressmaker's was just a week before the party. As soon as they arrived at Mrs Groves' salon, Harriet drew a note from her bag and asked for one of the seamstresses to deliver it to Mr Adcott's office for her.

'I hope he will agree to do a recitation for us,' she confided to Catherine. 'He has the most delightful bass voice. Something by Tennyson, perhaps.'

She smiled serenely as the dressmaker tightened the bodice, fastened the clasps, and finally stepped away to admire the finished gown.

'Quite delightful,' Mrs Groves enthused, clasping her lace-gloved hands together.

'Beautiful,' Catherine echoed, smiling as she watched Harriet turn to regard herself in the mirror. 'Your Papa will be so proud of you.'

'I shall have the gown boxed up and sent over to the Hall tomorrow morning,' Mrs Groves assured them. 'And I hope, if I may be so bold, it won't be long until I'm asked to create a wedding gown for a certain young lady.'

Harriet returned her smile steadily.

'I'm afraid we live a secluded life at Cropstone, Mrs Groves,' she said. 'We count few single gentlemen among our acquaintances. No, our party will comprise my dear cousins and aunts, and a few of my father's oldest friends.' Her glance strayed to Catherine Pendine. What was it in her gaze? Who was she thinking of? A handsome and most eligible batchelor not a few streets' distant from them?

The market clock chimed for midday as they returned to the street.

'I should like to spend a few minutes in the church,' Harriet said. 'If you'd be so kind as to deliver this note to my aunt?'

'I should accompany you,' Catherine began.

'I shall be perfectly safe in church until you return,' Harriet persuaded. 'It's almost six years since my mother died. I should like to offer my prayers in private.'

'Of course,' the governess said, bowing her head. She took the note Harriet gave her. Harriet watched her walk away, then, with brisk steps, she made her way into the churchyard.

She caught sight of him at once, standing between the gravestones like a statue himself, a tall thin young man, already slightly stooping from the hours he spent hunched over legal tomes.

'Mr Kendall,' she said. He turned, his pale face transformed with the light of his smile. He caught his hands anxiously together.

'M-Miss Dash,' he stammered. 'Y-your servant.' He made a stiff half bow. 'Your note spoke of a matter of grave concern, concerning Miss Pendine.'

'Indeed. A matter with which I think you are well acquainted, Mr Kendall.' She saw the blush suffuse his face. She was right. He knew Catherine Pendine's secret.

'I am privy to a great m-many matters,' he faltered, anguished. 'But you must understand, these are private affairs which I cannot divulge.'

'Of course,' she soothed. 'I hold you in too high a regard to think you might betray a confidence.'

His gaze drew back to her face, lingering there with a dogged devotion. She drew imperceptibly closer.

'I understand Miss Pendine left her previous post at very short notice due to a personal matter. I would only wish for reassurance that, if the facts surrounding such a matter were known, it would not reflect badly upon my own good name and reputation,' she said, her voice low, with just the slightest tremor to reflect the delicacy of her feelings. 'As you can appreciate, any taint or suspicion attaching to my governess would cast a shadow upon my own prospects.'

'My dear Miss Dash,' he responded, his eyes shining, 'You need have no fear in that respect. I believe Miss Pendine has behaved with utmost propriety, indeed, with generosity, towards her sister.'

'Her sister?'

'Miss Jane Pendine,' he said, in hushed confidential tones. 'A matter concerning her health, I understand.' He stood back a little, blushing all the more deeply. 'There, now I've said more than I should.'

'Not at all,' Harriet assured him. 'You merely sought to reassure me and I'm grateful for that,' she said. Her sister *'J'*, in Hereford. 'Most grateful.'

'Miss Dash …'

He made his bow but already she was turning away towards the church, her cheeks flaming, yet her skin was icy cold.

'My dearest Caro'. Of course. Not a lover at all. *'Propriety'* and *'generosity'* were not going to rid her of Catherine Pendine, she thought crossly. But there must be some way.

She halted, finding herself in the nave of the church. Before her rose the handsome stained glass window, the light flooding through to pool at her feet in sheens of rose and azure. How serene they looked, the richly coloured knights and princes. And how her thoughts whirled and churned like leaves in an autumn

102

gale. Yet how did her sister's welfare explain Catherine Pendine's visit to Robert Meredith? There had to be more to this, she concluded.

She sat, head bowed, in the nearest box pew, her fingers plied together as she desperately tried to untangle her best course.

'Miss Dash?'

She looked up in surprise at hearing her name. And saw Robert Meredith standing before her, that gleam in his eyes as brightly focused as a hound scenting its quarry.

'Forgive me,' he said. 'I don't wish to intrude upon your devotions, but you seem a little distressed. I hope everything is well with you?'

'Yes. Thank you,' she breathed, rising slowly. 'I came here to offer my prayers. It is the anniversary of my mother's death.'

'My condolences,' he said softly, his face stern yet with a gentleness in his eyes that she found both soothing and disturbing. Such a gaze. How compelling it was.

She inclined her head, her eyes downcast.

'Are you alone here in Ludlow, Miss Dash?'

'No. Miss Pendine is with me. My governess,' she said lightly. Of course he knew full well who Miss Pendine was. But would he admit as much to her? When she glanced at him again she could not read beyond the sparkle in his eyes. 'She'll be here directly.'

She found she was suddenly impatient for her governess's return. Despite the safety and sanctity of the high church walls around her, she felt intimidated by his gaze. There was something in the way he looked at her that made her feel as if her every thought and emotion stood in plain view before him, utterly naked.

'If you'll excuse me ...' she said, retreating from him. She clutched her hands together in a gesture of prayer, and sank, gratefully, into the safety of the pew once more.

She did not hear him go.

A whisper reached her, close by. She thought she heard his words, spoken very softly.

'To beauty sacred, and those angel eyes.'

She did not dare look round.

There were hurried footsteps then, and the brush of fabric over the stone floor, and looking up, she saw Catherine Pendine. The governess frowned. Her gaze dazzled with suspicion.

'You were alone here, Harriet?' she asked, in some agitation.

'Yes of course,' Harriet said, matching her enquiring stare with a ruthless calm.

'I thought I saw someone here.'

'If there was, I paid them no heed,' she said with a shrug. 'I was at prayer.'

Harriet patiently embroidered a lavender stem in neat satin stitch, in token of Samuel Kendall's devotion to her. He had proved himself every bit as useful as she had hoped. She tacked the hexagon shape around a paper piece on which was written a single word, *Jane*. Next she took a scrap of rose pink silk and cut from it a heart to stitch onto the patchwork piece. Whose heart? She had been convinced that 'J' had been Catherine Pendine's secret love. Now, she wondered if it was Robert Meredith the governess had set her cap at. Certainly, from the way he had looked at her in the church that day, he seemed to have little concern for a lowly governess. The recollection of their meeting sent her heartbeat racing. She had only to conjure those

104

eyes, the softness of his voice, to feel again that strange, compelling thrill run through her, as if her veins coursed with ice and fire together. A heart to represent love. Is that what she felt for him? And what of his feelings for her? There could be no doubt, surely, that his words had been a subtle declaration of his feelings. Concealed on the paper beneath the heart she had written the initials *R.M.* and remembered his soft words.

'To beauty sacred, and those angel eyes.'

She whispered them as she wrote them in tiny script upon the paper piece, and, with a tremor, folded his words in secret into the quilt, beneath the embroidered outline of a snowdrop. A snowdrop for hope.

All day the Hall had been in a flurry of preparation for the evening's dinner party. Flowers massed in tall vases, scented the reception rooms with the musky perfume of roses, and the sweet fragrance of lilies. The beeswax scent of the week's assiduous polishing lingered in the hall. In the kitchen and scullery, the maids had been working since dawn, straining and setting jellies and sauces, preparing pans of vegetables, trimming, basting and boiling the meats for the main courses, steaming puddings.

Alone in her room, Harriet sat serenely. She had practised her piano pieces to perfection: études by Chopin and Mozart, and her two songs, 'The Cuckoo' and 'Sweet and Low', to be accompanied by the governess. She turned one last time before her mirror, this way and that, rehearsing a smile, a simple curtsey, and then made her way downstairs to greet their guests.

'Charming. Quite charming,' her aunt enthused, catching her arm about her and kissing her cheek.

105

Isobel Lindley had her brother's tall, rather gaunt figure but her smile was broad and generous. 'My dear, you must come and meet Cousin Thomas. It's been so long since he last saw you. You visited Hopwood Hall when you were just a tiny thing, before your dear Mama became ill. Do you recall?' She steered Harriet past the vicar and his wife, and their awkward, bony headed young curate, to the straw-haired young man who stood at the mantelpiece, in conversation with Catherine Pendine. He had a long face with bulging brown eyes, and rather large ears, Harriet considered. His teeth, when he smiled, seemed to jut from his mouth. It gave him the look of hare, Harriet thought. She had no memory of him at all.

'Cousin Harriet, I should not have recognised you,' Thomas told her, bowing as he took her hand. 'Time has indeed worked her magic. Here you are, quite grown up, and how enchanting you look.' Harriet glanced impatiently at her aunt. Finally, she realised, the process was complete. All these weeks under her governess's tutelage, and now at last she had been brought to market. She was to be paraded and judged, and, if successful, would be rewarded with a marriage proposal. Her smile stiffened as she withdrew her hand from Cousin Thomas's damp grasp. She dipped a shallow curtsey to hide the momentary fury in her eyes.

'How kind of you to come and join our celebrations,' she said with little enthusiasm. 'I hope the journey was not too arduous for you.'

'It was most agreeable,' he assured her. 'It is but a short train journey from Hereford, and I'm staying for a few days with your aunt. She assures me I will find plenty to divert me in Ludlow.'

Harriet felt her heartbeat quicken. Her initial antipathy towards the young man was instantly

106

overwhelmed by a new urgency. Hereford. Of course. Catherine Pendine's previous position with the Oakleys had been in Hereford.

'I'm afraid I remember nothing of Hopwood Hall,' she said more warmly. She kept her gaze steadily upon his face, resisting the temptation to turn to see Catherine Pendine's reaction. 'I'm so glad we can renew our acquaintance now. I believe you have a very fine cathedral in Hereford.'

'Indeed we do,' he told her, smiling broadly, his face flushed with the unexpected warmth of her attention. 'And our house at Hopwood is reputed to be one of the best in the county.'

There was something in his look of almost canine devotion that reminded her of Samuel Kendall, the lawyer's clerk, she thought. She caught sight of her reflection in the gilt-framed mirror over the fireplace, and wondered what they saw when they looked at her. What did Robert Meredith see? Her beauty? Or her fortune? Her dark hair and oval face were handsome enough, and in her features she saw an echo of her mother's. Had her marriage been a happy one? She sighed.

'Dear Harriet,' her aunt whispered, catching her arm as she steered her towards more introductions. 'You seem to have made quite an impression on Thomas already. I do so hope you two will be friends. You recall his father died just a year ago. He has come into a considerable fortune.'

Harriet squeezed her aunt's hand and returned a smile. It was not Thomas's friendship she sought, and certainly not a proposal of marriage. She had no intention of leaving Cropstone yet. But friendship would be enough for now as she sought the means to oust Catherine Pendine from her home.

At last her father emerged from the library in the company of Lawyer Adcott, and escorted Harriet into dinner. She took her place at the head of the table, with her cousin Thomas to one side and the new curate on the other.

'Of course, Catherine, I'm sure, is very familiar with the cathedral at Hereford. You were previously engaged with a family there, were you not?' Harriet said, seizing the opportunity with relish.

'Yes,' Catherine said. She seemed agitated, Harriet saw with satisfaction. She saw the governess's fingers tighten around the fork she held. She put it down and patted at her lips with her napkin as if her appetite had suddenly deserted her. 'For two years, I was with Mr and Mrs Oakley. I believe their elder daughter is now married.'

Thomas Watkins nodded, but his attention was all on Harriet. Somehow she maintained a chatter of conversation between him and the curate, pretending an interest in church architecture and sacred music, impatient for the meal to be over so that she could concentrate on achieving her aim to visit Hereford in the very near future.

'Bravo,' Thomas, who had installed himself beside Harriet at the piano as her page-turner, clapped his hands together with enthusiasm as she completed her pieces. She looked for her father in the little crowd, and saw him give a solemn nod of approval. At least he had been listening.

As she rose, and made her curtsey, she was aware of Catherine Pendine approaching. The governess took her seat at the piano, and as she reached to open the pages of music, Harriet saw her father take Thomas's place at Catherine's side.

As the first few notes sounded, Catherine Pendine's clear voice began a plaintive country ballad. The audience hushed to listen. Harriet took in her father's tall, upright frame, beside the petite and slender figure of the governess. His face was turned to her, rapt with attention, and for the first time there seemed to be real animation in his eyes that had been frozen for so long.

Harriet's face burned. How could she not have realised before how fond her father had become of the governess, how he relied on her, sought her advice on his daughter's education. Catherine Pendine, with her shyness and deference, and her simpering smile, had wormed her way into his affections as easily as a knife cutting butter. How could she have been so blind all these weeks! How had she let herself become so obsessed with her plan to dislodge the governess, she had not seen Miss Pendine's own plot to secure a future for herself as William Dash's wife.

'She will make a laughing stock of me,' Harriet thought angrily. She glared at her father in icy hatred. How could he have been so foolish? Could he not see how the governess had manipulated him?

The notes rang out, halting at first, then with rising assurance, as William Dash joined in the chorus of the ballad.

'Who ever would have thought ...' the vicar's wife murmured to her husband, close by. 'What she's achieved with Miss Harriet, and now with the father ...'

Harriet turned and fled from the room, out into the hall, out through the front doors and down over the steps into the garden, escaping down the path into the Rose Walk as the light was fading, fleeing until the summerhouse came in view through the blur of her tears. There she halted, breathing hard, like a cornered fox.

She became aware then, above the drumming of her heart, that there were footsteps clipping towards her down the path.

She shut the door of the summerhouse and willed them to go by, keeping silent and still in the darkness. But they halted. The door squeaked open.

'Harriet?'

It was Thomas Watkins.

She caught her breath, fighting to still the tears.

'I'm sorry,' she whispered. 'It was foolish of me …
That song. It was a favourite of my mother's. To hear it sung now, by my father and my governess …'

'It's all right. I understand,' he said. 'Here.' He offered her his handkerchief. She took it timidly, touched it to her face. It smelt vaguely of roses. An unwelcome reminder of the governess. She bit back her fury and thrust the handkerchief back at him.

'There. I'm quite recovered, thank you,' she said. 'We should go back indoors. They'll be looking for us.'

'They're enjoying the music,' he said. 'Besides, since you showed such an interest in our cathedral at Hereford, I came to ask if you wished to spend a few days with us at Hopwood next week. We're holding our annual fête.'

'Oh. Next week?' She took courage from the unexpected opportunity. 'Yes. If Papa will give permission, then, yes, I should like that very much,' she told him eagerly.

'Good. That's settled then.' He held open the door, and offered her his arm.

As she stepped forward, he took her gloved hand in his and drew it to his lips and held it there.

She wanted to pull her hand away, but knew she dared not risk losing him as an ally. Not yet at least. She stared up at him, her breath coming fast, anxious for escape.

'I did not lie when I said how beautiful I thought you,' he murmured. 'I am, truly, enchanted,' he said, and drawing her closer to him, he bowed his head and gently kissed her. She felt her lips bump against his teeth, felt the damp press of his hand through the silk of her gown, and shuddered.

She closed her eyes, her fingers clenching on his arm, as he kissed her again, this time with more fervour, and found herself conjuring quite a different face. With dark, compelling eyes, and straight dark brows, and those softly spoken words.

'*To beauty sacred, and those angel eyes.*'

She felt a betraying shiver. She must not think of Robert Meredith, she told herself. Think only of Catherine Pendine. She remembered the way her father had looked at the governess. Much the same way Robert Meredith had looked at her in the church in Ludlow: a look of hunger that would not long be resisted.

She realised she was still enfolded in Thomas's embrace. She hastily drew back from him with a little cry of alarm. In the darkness his smile widened, encouraged by her acquiescence.

'I do so look forward to renewing our friendship at Hopwood, Harriet dearest.'

Next morning as she sat calmly at her embroidery, Harriet gave no outward sign of the turmoil in her heart. While Catherine Pendine practised a new piano piece, Harriet bent over her embroidery, working the shapes of music notes onto the patchwork pieces to remind her of the humiliation of the previous evening, and of the fury she had felt the moment she realised what Catherine Pendine had been planning all these weeks. The peony she stitched was composed of pink petals, satin stitched, and at their heart, a thick clutch of French knots to form stamens. The peony was a symbol of anger and indignation. On the next piece, she stitched a buttercup for the pursuit of riches. She knew now that if she failed to get rid of her, Catherine Pendine would soon be her stepmother.

'Miss Harriet, Mr Kendall has come from the lawyers,' Annie said, coming into the room with the young clerk's business card. 'Your father's not back yet from his ride. Should I ask him to wait?'

'I'll see him myself,' Harriet told her. Catherine paused from her playing, but said nothing. Moments later her playing resumed, though at a slower tempo as if distracted.

'Mr. Kendall, I'm sorry my father is not here,' Harriet said, closing the drawing room door behind her, muting the music. Samuel looked dismayed, clutching to his hat as he watched her approach.

'Your father did ask for the papers to be brought as soon as they were ready for him to sign, but since he's not here ...'

'If you'd care to leave the papers with me, I'll see that he gets them upon his return.'

'They should be w-witnessed,' he said, avoiding her sharp gaze.

'Witnessed?' Her gaze narrowed. What legal documents required a signature so urgently?

'If I may, I shall await his return.'

'There's no need,' she said coolly, and with a reassuring smile, held out her hand for the document he carried. He hesitated, shifting uneasily from foot to foot.

'Miss D-Dash, my instructions …' he began.

'Kendall, there you are! Come on in to the library,' William Dash said, striding into the hall, still in his muddied outdoor boots, with the dogs panting at his heels, his face crimsoned from the June sun. 'Ask Mrs Warren to step in, would you, Harriet?'

'Yes Papa.'

Two witnesses. He was changing his will. It had to be, she thought angrily as she rang for the housekeeper. And Catherine Pendine, she had no doubt, was at the root of it. This was all for her benefit.

'And where exactly does that leave me?' she thought angrily.

After lunch, William Dash retreated to the library, the door closed. Harriet paced restlessly across the hall. There was nothing for it. She had to know. Softly she knocked and went in.

'Papa, might I borrow one of the books on flowers for my studies?'

He was sitting in the wing chair by the fire, a slim volume of poetry open in his hands, but his eyes were reddened from sleep.

'Yes, yes of course,' he said thickly.

He looked weary, she thought. Perhaps she shouldn't have disturbed him.

'You take a keen interest in the outdoors, picking flowers and such?' he remarked.

'Yes, Papa. I enjoy studying their shapes and colours.'

He gave an approving grunt. 'Well, there's no harm in botany.'

'I prefer it to playing the piano,' she said, rolling the library steps towards the shelf where his collection of books on flora were kept.

'Nonetheless, that's a skill that has its uses too. And your playing certainly impressed your cousin Thomas. I hear you've an invitation to visit.' He studied her a moment, his eyes shining. 'My sister considers him a most agreeable young man. I own, I'd not be sorry to see our two families more closely tied,' he said softly. 'His father was a great horseman. Kept a fine stable. If the boy's inherited half his horse-sense, he won't go far wrong.'

Harriet kept very still, her eyes downcast, hardly breathing as she took in what her father said. Slowly the colour rose in her cheeks. Was it all settled then? Was she to have no say in her own future?

He set down his book on the small table at his elbow. 'Your fortune is secure, Harriet, you know that. You have a trust worth a thousand a year once you are of age, and there's a generous dowry upon your marriage. You don't have to accept Thomas. You can marry where you will. Provided the match has my approval, of course,' he added.

'Thank you Papa,' she said, her throat constricted with the grip of anger and fear. She turned away from him, her fingers reaching along the familiar volumes.

'Of course, upon your engagement, Miss Pendine's post as your governess will cease,' he said, clearing his throat. 'She has grown so much a part of our home now, I have it in mind to ask her to join us in a more permanent position.'

She glanced down at him from her perch on the library steps. There it was again, that look almost of hunger.

'We've no need of a new housekeeper,' she said tartly.

'I had in mind a more intimate role,' he said. 'I've asked her to be my wife.'

She turned her face from him, glaring furiously at the rows of leather clad spines, the gilt letters blurring before her. Her trembling fingers reached hesitantly, then with more certainty, and prised out a volume: '*A Herbal of Garden and Woodland Plants*'.

Carefully she descended the steps, clutching the volume to her chest. 'I'm sure whatever you decide will be for the best, Papa,' she said, her cheeks reddening. 'And I'm sure I shall be very happy as Thomas's wife.'

In the safety of the summerhouse, far away from prying eyes, Harriet opened the book she had glimpsed once before. She had found the etched drawings dull, and the text read more like a cookbook. So many recipes: syrups and decoctions, plasters, preserves and poultices, electuaries and oils. How to cure toothache, what's best for stopping cuts. Impatiently she turned the pages, seeking the chapter that had both alarmed and fascinated her as a child: *Poisonous Plants*.

The tight frown across her brow eased as she smiled. She had no intention of Catherine Pendine usurping her place at Cropstone Hall. One way or another, she would be rid of her.

Harriet retreated to her room after dinner to embark on a methodical study, listing which parts of the plant were to be used, when they should be harvested, and which methods should be employed to extract their power. It seemed that the fields and woodlands around the Hall, and even their own flower gardens, offered an abundant choice of poisons, like the Devil's own pantry. She had never before suspected the true dangers locked within the tempting apple, for at its heart were pips that could be crushed to make the potent poison, cyanide.

Her appreciative glance lingered on the sinister beauty of the fungi depicted in the pages. How handsome was the deadly Fly Agaric, and the virginally white Destroying Angel. Pity it was not the season for mushrooms, she thought.

The June days meant most plants in the garden and the woodlands around were now in flower. Though there were no berries as yet, still their roots and leaves would be easy to gather, and with the rising sap of summer, they would likely be at their most potent. That, in itself, she saw might pose a problem. She had no wish to kill the governess outright. There was every likelihood she would be discovered as her killer. No, she had to proceed with utmost caution.

She envisaged more of a slow decline, much as her mother had dwindled over years until her ultimate death. Perhaps a few lapses into ill health would be sufficient reminder of all her mother had suffered for her father to abandon all thought of marriage. She would need to make a careful study to select the perfect poison.

'Christmas,' she thought, snapping the book shut. 'Now there's a time for poisons.' With all those deadly berries brought innocently into the house for decoration: ivy and mistletoe, even the merry Christmas holly with its handsome berries. Such potential for harm. She pictured a berried sprig speared in the top of one of Cook's plum puddings. A strange celebration indeed.

Harriet paced the length of the flower garden the next morning with a keener than usual interest, admiring the ribbon of bedding plants the gardeners had so diligently planted. But it was not the beauty of form of colour that attracted her. She thought only of the book hidden in her room, with its illustrations of nodding hellebore with roots that could be used as a powerful emetic, and a potential to be fatal. Then there were the golden trumpets of daffodils. Yet the opportunity of introducing a bulb in mistake for an onion was remote. Mrs Marsh kept too close a watch on her kitchen, and Harriet had never before shown the slightest interest in its mysterious processes. She had to keep her part in Miss Pendine's demise well concealed. Besides, it would be almost impossible to poison one of them at the table without harming herself or her father. She smiled, recalling her father's words.

'There is,' he had said, 'no harm in botany'.

She returned to the schoolroom with her first collection to study, and set the hellebore leaves and the foxglove spire in a jug of water while she fetched her sketchbook and watercolours. The governess bowed over her shoulder as she painted.

'I've decided to make a botanic study of the estate,' Harriet told her. 'It's an interest Cousin Thomas shares.'

Catherine, with a murmured approval, left her to her work. Harriet slid out her book from beneath her watercolour page and studied how best to derive a poison from the leaves and flowers she had gathered. Diligently, she made notes which she folded away beneath her apron to study later in her room. Page by page, with notes and sketches, she would devise her own handbook of poisons.

*

117

Through the heat of the June morning, the cream and brown liveried Great Western Railway train huffed its way along the winding river valley, from Craven Arms through Onibury, Ludlow and Leominster to Hereford. Harriet, seated beside Annie, admired from the carriage window the golden meadows. With delight she remembered, from her reading, how even the humble meadow buttercup, Ranunculus acris, if eaten, could cause blisters of the mouth, stomach pains, and ultimately, could kill.

As the train rattled on its journey, the plant names pulsed in her head in a strangely soothing litany: ranunculus and mistletoe, hellebore, hemlock, laburnum, aconitum. So many to choose from. But which one would ultimately assure the governess's demise?

The sudden roar and shush of steam and sparks roused her from her dark thoughts. They had arrived at last in Hereford. Peering through the dissipating cloud of steam, she caught sight of Thomas Watkins waiting for them on the platform with his man.

'Dear Harriet, what a joy it is to welcome you,' he professed as she stepped down from the train. Glancing past her, he caught sight of her maid, Annie. 'What, no governess with you?'

Harriet gave a shy smile.

'Sadly, no. She felt unwell as we were travelling to the station and had to return home with Purslow.'

'No matter,' he breezed. His smile broadened as he drew her arm through his to escort her through the little crowd on the platform, leaving Annie and his man to gather up their luggage. 'You're here, and that's all the matters. Come, this way. We're but a short carriage ride out of the town.'

Her recollections of Hopcroft Hall were scant. She could have been no more than five years old on her last visit. She remembered the Watkins' nursery as a bleak grey room, with a tall doll's house she had thought the most magical creation, with its own little world created within.

On the Hall steps, Mrs Watkins was waiting to greet her, a large fleshy woman in the grey silks and jade beads of half-mourning.

'Thomas told me what a beauty you'd become,' she enthused, clasping Harriet's small hand in a surprising vigorous embrace. 'I can see your poor Mama in your face. How is your Papa bearing up?' she asked her, ushering her indoors.

'Well enough, thank you,' Harriet told her, and refrained from adding that he was sufficiently recovered from his grief to be set on marrying the governess. Her maid, Annie, was dispatched with their luggage to unpack.

'The governess is not come, Mama,' Thomas informed his mother.

'Indeed? You have travelled alone?'

'With Annie,' Harriet said. 'I did not wish to disappoint you ... and I have been so looking forward to our visit,' she told her. 'Miss Pendine was taken with stomach cramps on our way to the station and had to return home.'

Mrs Watkins nodded wisely.

'It can be most incapacitating,' she confided. 'I can recommend warm milk and ginger. I always found it most soothing.'

'Thank you,' Harriet said, blushing a little. She had her own opinion as to the source of Miss Pendine's discomfort. She had hidden one of the foxglove leaves in her skirt pocket that morning and gently wiped it around the rim of Miss Pendine's teacup. Not enough to cause serious harm, but a little discomfort was a promising start to her project.

'I'm sure your Papa will miss you. It must have been a blessing to him in his time of sorrow to have you near him,' Mrs Watkins was saying. 'You remember Eugenia, my daughter? It's years since you two were play-fellows.'

Mrs Watkins introduced the haughty young woman who came to greet her.

Harriet summoned a taut smile. Oh yes, she remembered Eugenia very well. Some four years her senior, it had been her doll's house Harriet had admired. And she had complained that Harriet had broken some of the furniture with her clumsy eager fingers, and so had banned her from playing with it again. After tea, when the children had been ushered down from the nursery by their nannies to be inspected by the grown-ups, it was Eugenia, standing just behind her, who had tired of Mrs Watkins' praise of Harriet's angelic face and luxuriant curls, and had pinched her arm hard. Harriet's resultant tears had seen them all dismissed swiftly back to the nursery. But not before Harriet had seen her mother's pale face pinched with anguish, and her father's condemning frown. No, Harriet remembered Eugenia very well. Though judging from the young woman's vapid smile she had no recollection of Harriet at all.

'Dear Eugenia has been married these past two years,' she said, bestowing a doting smile on the young woman. Eugenia, her hand straying to the prominent mound of her stomach, smiled back. 'Ah, I should dearly love to see Thomas settled,' Mrs Watkins went on. 'With a wife and family of his own. He is such a kind boy.'

'Can't wait to show you round our stables,' Thomas said, beaming at her, the sunlight gleaming on his hare like teeth.

'Stables?' Harriet faltered.

'Horses!' he said proudly. 'The finest. As you will soon have the opportunity of witnessing. Our fête tomorrow will be a very special day. Three races, and the third of them will be a special race, run in my father's honour: the Sir William Watkins plate. It's for gentleman riders, and we've a prize of twenty guineas.'

'Indeed?' she said, trying to summon some enthusiasm. Carriage beasts or plough animals were all very well but horses, in her experience, were bad-tempered and unreliable, and she had never been able to fathom her father's obsession with them.

'Thomas, you must allow our dear guest a little time to recover from her journey. I'll have our maid show you up to you room. Do join us as soon as you are rested,' Mrs Watkins encouraged her. 'We dine at five.'

Harriet took her chance for escape gladly. She found Annie waiting for her, her clothes already unpacked. The room was much as she expected: rather dark, with elaborately patterned paper and tapestried curtains, and filled with large cumbersome furniture of considerable age. She wondered where the doll's house was now. She gave Annie a weak smile, and tried to pretend enthusiasm, on her guard now to keep her true motives for her visit to Hopwood concealed. Servants, no matter how loyal, could betray her with an unwary word.

'Can you imagine? This could one day be my home.'

Thankfully the preparations for the day's festivities meant Harriet was spared much of Thomas's company.

She sat with Mrs Watkins and a taciturn Eugenia and listened to the catalogue of Thomas's skills and accomplishments, and an eager exposition of Eugenia's husband's gallantry and importance to the nation's safety, for he was with his regiment on the south coast and unable to join them.

By midday, the lawn in front of the Hall had been set with long trestle tables covered with white cloths. Under the sharp instructions of butler and housekeeper, a relay of servants carried out dishes of gammon, pies and cheeses. Kegs of ale and jugs of lemonade were brought out ready for the celebrations. A jumble of musicians were sorting out tubas and bassoons, trying a few discordant notes that gradually congealed into a thumping tune as the grounds filled with people from the villages and farms around, in carts and traps or on foot.

Harriet took her place in one of the open carriages next to the racecourse, sheltered from the heat of the June sun under white parasols. The course was marked out with a series of poles, looping out across the parkland, over low hedges into the adjacent fields, then back to finish before the crowd on the lawn: a chase of some three miles in all, Thomas had told her.

'My dear husband loved these race days,' Mrs Watkins told her. 'This is the first one since his passing. Thomas has been so looking forward to it. And of course to sharing it with our special guest,' she said with a meaningful smile.

Harriet's smile was less enthusiastic. Her glance slid to Eugenia and saw the woman's sly look, just the same as the day she had pinched her to make her cry. A prospect of buttercups filled her mind. A little discomfort would make up for the pain Eugenia had made her suffer as children.

From the direction of the stableyard, through the milling crowd, the first string of horses emerged. Sons of the local farmers, mostly, and a few tradesmen from the town, Mrs Watkins said, pointing out the more worthy, or wealthy, among them.

Thomas waved to them from the starter's chair. Moments later a man in a bowler raised a flag, the milling horses were urged and cajoled to all face more or less in the same direction, and, as the flag dropped, they sprang away into a gallop across the park.

By the time of the third race, the crowd had grown noisier and more boisterous, inspired by the copious beer and the fine weather. The strains of brassy music dipped and swelled on the warm breeze. Harriet strained to see Thomas at the starter's chair, but there was no sign of him.

'There, look, there he is!' Eugenia said eagerly. Harriet could see him now, at the head of the next batch of riders, dressed in a hunting jacket and breeches.

'He's racing?' Harriet said.

'Of course. He wouldn't miss this for the world.'

Harriet stood up in the carriage and waved to him. He returned her wave with a nod, touching his hat brim with his riding crop. It was then she caught sight of the rider close beside him.

She sat down abruptly, her cheeks scarlet. There was no mistaking those dark eyes, the straight dark brows. As he saw her, the muscles tightened in his face. Then he was lost in the throng and she stared straight ahead of her, afraid of meeting his eyes again. What had brought Robert Meredith there?

With a tumult of shouts and cries, the horses thundered off at a gallop. Harriet stood to watch them go, saw the bunching bodies crowd towards the hedge, the flailing hooves as they jumped. All were over safely, heading towards the next hedge across the field. She could hardly breathe.

'They've turned … look, I think it's Thomas in the lead!' Eugenia cried.

Harriet shaded her eyes against the sun, straining to see as the leading riders galloped full tilt towards the hedge that would bring them back into the park.

'There are two of them, neck and neck. I can't make out which is Thomas,' Harriet said, her stomach clenched with alarm at the speed they were careering towards the hedge.

As they steadied to jump, Harriet saw a sudden glint of sunlight. Seconds later, one of the horses stumbled, somehow launched itself across the hedge but fell heavily, sending its rider tumbling to the ground. Harriet gasped.

'It's Thomas!'

The leading rider galloped on towards them, raising his hand to the cheers of the crowd. Harriet had already jumped down from the carriage and was running through the field to where Thomas lay. There were others with him now, helping him to sit. He bowed his head groggily. How pale he looked, she thought in alarm.

'How is he? Is he all right?' she gasped as she reached them.

'Winded, I think,' said one of the men who was kneeling beside him. 'No bones broken.'

'Thank God,' she whispered. She took a step backwards, feeling suddenly faint beneath the glare of the sun, the press of the crowd. She felt someone's hand at her waist, supporting her. She swung round and met Robert Meredith's eyes.

'To the victor the spoils,' he murmured.

'He could have been killed,' she said furiously. She shrugged away his touch and dropped to her knees beside Thomas and reached for his hand.

Thomas opened his eyes and looked blearily up at her.

'Dear Harriet, I so wanted to win for you.'

Thomas was duly carried back indoors and examined by the doctor who, in due course, announced that, apart from bruising and a swollen knee, he was unharmed.

'I recommend a few days' rest,' the doctor informed the anxious family. 'And poultices for his knee.'

'A poor host, I've been for you,' Thomas told Harriet ruefully when at last he was allowed to see his visitor in his room, accompanied by his sister and mother. 'I promise to make it up to you as soon as I'm well again.'

'You must rest. Dr Carter was most insistent,' his mother warned. 'Harriet will not want for company or entertainment while she is with us. Will you, my dear?'

The following morning, Thomas was brought downstairs to sit on the terrace with the ladies. His ribs were bruised and aching, and his knee was still very swollen and pained him, but he was in good spirits. All the more so when the maid announced their visitor's arrival.

'My dear Thomas, I can't tell you how sorry I am. Are you truly recovering?' Robert Meredith greeted the invalid as he strode across the terrace to join them.

Harriet stiffened at the sound of his voice. She kept her gaze downcast on her hands folded in her lap.

'It'll be but a few days till I'm back in the saddle,' Thomas assured him. 'And thankfully Diamond is no worse for his tumble.'

'A great horse. Great spirit,' Robert said.

'But I fear I'm a poor host for our guest,' Thomas said.

Only now did Meredith look to where Harriet sat, her gaze downcast, at Mrs Watkins' side.

'I'm sure Miss Dash has no complaints.'

'But I had promised her a visit to the cathedral.'

Meredith smiled, made a bow towards the ladies.

'Then I would be glad to escort them, if you'd permit me. I'm not due back in Ludlow for a few days yet.'

'I couldn't possibly …' Harriet began fearfully, but already arrangements were being made. Eugenia was to accompany her, together with her maid.

'I look forward to being at your service,' he said.

'What happened?' Harriet demanded fiercely as they stood together in the nave of the cathedral the next afternoon. Eugenia, in her delicate condition, walked more slowly behind them, supported by the maid, fanning herself after the heat out of doors. Glad of the cathedral's cool interior, she sank at once into one of the pews.

Meredith tilted back his head to peer up at the carvings of the roof vault, his hand extended as if pointing out to her some feature of interest.

'Happened? I don't know what you mean.'

'I saw a flash of light,' she hissed at him.

'Ah.' His gaze returned to her, then danced on past to where Eugenia sat, just out of earshot. He bowed his head to her, smiling. Turning away he strolled towards the tall pillars. 'Perhaps it was the ring I wore,' he said.

She looked down at his hands as he spread his fingers and saw the narrow band set with a small diamond. Her glare was no less fierce. 'The reflection may have dazzled him for a moment. Watkins mistimed the jump, that's all. Happens to the best of us.'

'You could have killed him.'

'Thomas is an experienced rider,' he dismissed. 'It's not the first time he's taken a tumble.'

She felt a shiver run through her as he spoke. Something in the way he phrased the words, the way he looked at her, as if he had quite some other meaning, quite some other picture in his mind. She turned back to Eugenia, moving briskly away from him.

'It's a most beautiful screen,' she said. 'Do you feel recovered enough to walk further?'

'It's most kind of you to accompany us,' Eugenia told Meredith as he caught up with them. 'I think it's time we returned to keep Thomas company.'

Meredith escorted them out of the cathedral, lightly supporting Eugenia's arm as they made their way through the churchyard. There was a neat row of almshouses, their small gardens brimming with flowers. Beyond, a fine stone house looked across the cloisters. The sign on the gate read, 'Belmont House'.

Harriet stopped, her brow creasing with a frown. Eugenia glanced back, conscious she was not following them.

'Harriet, are you all right?'

'Just the heat … after the cool of the cathedral,' she said, fanning herself rapidly. 'What is that place?' she asked.

'Oh, it's one of Mama's projects,' Eugenia said lightly. 'She's a patron. It's a home for governesses who are too old to work or between posts and find themselves in temporary distress. They busy themselves with needlework and such like.'

Belmont House. Harriet remembered where she had seen the name before. On a letter to Catherine Pendine, from her sister Jane. Was that the 'family matter' that had driven Catherine from her last post? An urgent need to find accommodation for her sister? She had a sense then of just how much a marriage to someone like William Dash would mean to the governess: a home and a fortune and security for both herself and her sister. Freedom from worry and the shame of poverty. How desperate she must be to secure him for her husband.

'You have a fine garden here,' she told Mrs Watkins as they sat in wicker chairs on the lawn behind the house, enjoying the fine summer afternoon. The wide flower borders brimmed with their bounty of paeonies, delphiniums and hollyhocks. Rambling roses cascaded in a flowery tumble from the trellis supports. 'I have a keen interest in botany. In fact, I'm making a study of the flora at Cropstone.'

'All that concerns me is the quality of the grass and the oats – for the horses,' Thomas brayed.

Meredith was announced, and invited to join them to take tea.

'I'm most grateful to you for escorting the ladies yesterday,' Thomas told him.

'My pleasure,' Meredith said. Neither he nor Harriet dared exchange a glance. 'I was admiring your garden, Mrs Watkins. I must take notes for my own place at Radnor.'

'Harriet can tell you more about the flowers. She's a student of botany,' Thomas said. 'I told her I'm more for grass and oats, for the horses,' he said and laughed again.

128

'Miss Dash?' Meredith turned to her, an eyebrow raised as if inviting her company, but it was Eugenia who got awkwardly to her feet.

'Allow me to give you a guided tour, Mr Meredith,' she said with a glance at her mother. 'I'm sure I'm more closely acquainted with our garden than our visitor.' She threaded her arm through Meredith's, shepherding him away from Harriet.

'Should we not have a botanist to guide us?' he said easily, pausing to wait as Harriet, blushing, rose to join them.

They strolled together over the grass, following the sinuous curve of the border. Harriet paused to admire the handsome spikes of blue monkshood flowers, aware that the aconite it contained was a deadly poison, that even a careless touch could bring harm. And what of the poppies? She loved to paint their crumpled petals and pepper pot seed heads, but the opium poppy held the potential to induce the deepest of sleeps. And the hedges of yew and laurel, too, would have berries that contained sufficient poison to be sure of dispensing death.

A narrow tiled path strayed off beyond the clipped yew hedge.

'Isn't that the stumpery? I remember your late father telling me about it. He was proud of its design,' Meredith said. 'I think such a feature would be the very thing for my garden. And I'm sure you'd find its shade welcome on such a day.'

Eugenia smiled, flattered at his concern for her condition, and led him along the path, with Harriet following in their wake.

The steepening path wound between high banks of soil stacked with upturned tree roots. Between the spikes of wood grew ferns and mosses, and over all was a scent of damp and decay. At a turn, Harriet lost sight of Meredith. She saw an arch of pebbles that marked the entrance to a grotto, little more than a dark shadowed cleft in the bank. She heard the scuff of a footstep in the gloom and halted.

'Eugenia?' she said uncertainly.

At once she felt strong hands around her waist, then the press of Meredith's face against hers, his lips seeking her mouth.

'There,' he said, his grip relaxing just enough to let her catch her breath. 'I have my answer.'

'Allow me to know the question,' she faltered, breathing hard.

'I wasn't sure until now how you felt about me,' he whispered. 'Now I know the truth.' His fingers touched her cheek, trailed down across her chin, to her throat, her neck. She stood as if trapped before him, unable, unwilling, to move. She felt the cold hard stones of the wall at her back.

'You must let me go,' she whispered, panic fluttering in her heart.

'So you can escape to Thomas?'

'He's your friend too. Yet you betray him by your conduct.'

'And you? Is your acquiescence not betrayal?'

She could feel his breath on her cheek. Still the panic drummed within her yet she sought his touch, wanted him to hold her there and press her to him.

'Harriet? Harriet, where are you?' Eugenia called out crossly.

'We must go. Eugenia will find us,' she said in alarm.

'She's all right,' Meredith called back. 'She's just slipped.' His mouth closed once more against hers as he whispered, 'Taken a tumble ...' As he kissed her, she

130

pressed against him, her arms lifting around his neck. She drank in the taste, the scent of him, willing him never to let her go.

'Harriet, are you all right?'

'Yes … quite …' she said breathless. Eugenia stood at the opening of the grotto, peering blindly into the darkness. 'So silly of me,' she said. 'I missed my footing.'

'The stones are quite slippery there,' Meredith said, supporting her by the arm as they stepped out into the light once more.

Eugenia's glance was cool with suspicion.

'We must rejoin the others,' she said tartly. 'They'll be wondering where we've got to.'

'You cannot go to him,' Meredith told Harriet in a hushed urgent tone as they made their slow way back across the garden, Harriet feigning the slightest of limps as if her ankle pained her.

'There is an understanding between our two families,' she hissed back.

'But is that what you want? To devote your life to Thomas and his horses? And to his horse-faced mother?'

She glanced to where Thomas sat watching them, saw his long hare like face, the protruding teeth as he gave a wide unsuspecting smile. Saw Mrs Watkins' imperious gaze upon them.

'What choice do I have?' she answered softly.

The carriage had been ordered to take Harriet back to the station the next morning. She had done her utmost to allay Mrs Watkins' evident suspicions about her growing attachment to Robert Meredith, and at dinner had endured Thomas's tales of hunts and horses with an attentive smile, all the while remembering the way

Meredith had looked at her, recalling the heat on her skin as he had touched her, the press of his lips.

But the problem of the governess had still to be resolved. Just what was the link between him and Catherine Pendine? Was it possible they had been lovers?

'Botany,' Mrs Watkins had said with a derisive sniff, as Eugenia had enquired after Harriet's ankle at dinner. 'I find there is plenty of charitable work here to occupy my time more fruitfully than in studying plants.'

Her mention of her charitable work had given Harriet the idea.

'Eugenia told me you're a patron of Belmont House. I should dearly like to see the work they do there. Of course I'm sure Papa will provide a pension for my own governess upon my marriage, or perhaps find work for her somewhere on the estate, but I am conscious that not all are so fortunate. Do you think I might call there on my way to the station tomorrow?'

'You do us a great honour,' Mrs Franklin, the stooped and grey-haired warden welcomed them, escorting Harriet and her maid through the gloomy building that belied the beauty of its name. 'We're most grateful to Mrs Watkins and her family for their generosity in supporting our ladies at their time of greatest need.'

'Perhaps I could meet one or two of your residents?' she asked the warden, conscious that she had little time before her train was due and she must return to Cropstone with a plan in place to remove Catherine Pendine from her life.

'With pleasure,' Mrs Franklin said, though her thin smile betrayed little affinity with that emotion. 'Here's the salon where many of our inmates sit during the day.

As you see they are all well cared for and contented.'

The residents sat either side a long table, busy with their needlework. Harriet looked at the row of grave and wrinkled faces upturned to her. She glanced round at the high plain walls. An austere room, she thought, without paintings or decoration. A small vase of wilting Sweet William on the mantelpiece struggled to bring a little cheer to the gaunt surroundings.

'Miss Gregg is our oldest resident. She's been with us for over six years now,' the warden confided.

Harriet gave a dutiful smile and admired the minutely stitched handkerchief the woman held up for her inspection, her grey eyes blinking behind round pebble glasses.

'Ah, and here is our newest resident, Miss Pendine. She joined us in April,' Mrs Franklin said. She halted half way down the row and gave a tight smile. 'See, Jane, you have a visitor.'

The woman glanced up, frowning, her pale wispy hair falling over her brow.

'Has my sister sent for me?' she asked in an urgent whisper.

Harriet felt her stomach tighten. She could see the resemblance at once to Catherine Pendine, but Jane was much older, thinner. Her grey eyes looked timidly up, seeking reassurance yet fearing she would find none, like a dog that is used to being beaten.

'Miss Jane Pendine?' Harriet made a show of surprise. 'I believe my governess, Catherine, is your sister.'

'Caro? Why, yes. Has she sent for me?' she asked again more anxiously, her fingers fretting over the handkerchief she had been stitching.

'She had a position in Brittany,' Mrs Franklin confided, 'Teaching English to a young French family.

133

I fear it took a toll upon her nerves. Their customs are sadly much different to our own. She was greatly perturbed when her sister brought her here to us, but I'm pleased to say she is much calmer now.'

'I trust she'll find another post soon,' Harriet said, in some alarm at the obviously precarious state of Jane Pendine's health.

The warden sighed. 'I fear she will not find work as a governess again. It's as well her sister is able to help support her.'

'Indeed,' Harriet said. How ever did Catherine Pendine manage to find any money to spare on the meagre salary she received? But then, Catherine Pendine had every expectation of finding a more lucrative position very soon. As Mrs William Dash.

Harriet bent and touched the woman's bony hand.

'I'm sure your sister will visit you soon,' she assured her.

As Jane Pendine looked up again and smiled, Harriet caught her breath. For a moment she could see in the calm radiance of her face the beauty she must once have been.

5

BRON

Friday morning

I blamed Vi of course. It was her idea that saw me heading back through Edgton next morning to snoop round Cropstone Hall in the hope of finding some clue as to where Caitlin had disappeared to. Since she'd left my cottage early on Wednesday morning, there'd been no word from her. No-one, other than Clive, seemed to have seen her. And now there was the added worry of the murdered girl, Nicky Price, whose body had been dumped at Bury Ditches. What if we had a serial killer at loose among these quiet lanes and secret valleys?

I parked the Land Rover in the lane near the old railway station at Horderley. All that remained now of the track from Craven Arms to Bishops Castle was an overgrown strip of seedling trees and bramble beside the winding riverbank. Clipping on William's lead, we started up the waymarked path that led along the hill behind Cropstone Hall.

Up through the fields, the track skirted the woods. Rooks cawed protectively over their cluster of nests in the fresh leaved branches. At that season, the air was sweet with the scent from the creamy hawthorn blossom and honeysuckle. The glossy petals of celandines sparkled among the new ferns and pale primroses. White wood anemones shone in the shadows under the trees. I took some photos. I thought of creating a tapestry effect of the woodland flowers in a quilt. As I tucked my camera back into my bag, I heard the thud of hoof beats approaching along the track behind me. I turned, screwing up my eyes against the sunlight.

The huge chestnut horse was reined back to a more sedate walk, despite the protesting shake of its head and a disdaining snort.

'I thought it was your car in the lane,' the rider called out.

I recognised Gabriel Haywood and my cheeks burned. I felt like a trespasser, caught in the searchlights. My mouth opened, but I couldn't find any words that would explain my presence there. Nothing that would deflect the suspicion I saw in his frown.

He was distracted then, tussling with the horse's head, the creature impatient at having its morning ride interrupted. I just hoped it wouldn't step on William who was sniffing round its hooves.

'William needed a walk,' I said, plunging into the first excuse I could think of. 'I've not been round here before. It's lovely,' I said lamely.

'It's a beautiful spot, isn't it?' His glance swung past me, across the valley, to the enclosing hills. 'Actually I was going to ring you,' he said. I found myself somewhat mesmerised by the well-muscled thighs outlined by his tight jeans. And blushed again as our eyes met.

'You were?' I stammered.

His smile broadened.

'I spoke to Lydia yesterday. Told her about the quilt. She reminded me, we did find something when the place was being renovated. I've looked it out for you. Why don't you come on down to the house for a coffee? I'll go on ahead and get Monty back to the stables.'

I stood watching as he touched his boot heel to the horse's glossy flank, and set off past me at a rising trot, and that awesome view of his neat backside.

'Well, William,' I said breathlessly, bending to scratch the little dog's ears. 'I'm relying on you to keep your eyes and ears open for any sign of Cat.'

He gave an excited yap.

'No,' I sighed. 'Caitlin.'

I set off along the track with the dog. Perhaps I shouldn't rely too much on canine instinct.

Gabriel was just emerging from the tack room by the time I reached the gate. Already Monty had been turned out into the paddock to graze, and gave only the slightest roll of his eyes as the little dog came into view.

'Guided tour first,' Gabriel said. 'The walled garden's this way.'

The arched wooden door opened onto a square of close-mown lawn, disappointingly unlike the secret garden of my childhood imaginings. In the old brickwork there were ghosts of past horticulture: vestiges of whitewash on the brickwork and the traces of the brick base of a glasshouse, vine eyes where once wires had been stretched to support espalier fruit trees. In one corner was an ancient rose bush, fiercely trimmed. I gazed up at the bricks, already imagining recreating their pattern and texture in fabric, with a gauze of thread perhaps for branches.

'Thought I might make a tennis court of it,' Gabriel said. I didn't tell him about the patchwork. I wondered what Ed would have made of it, with his flair for garden design. I could imagine the pained look on his face, the almost apoplectic splutter of outrage.

'Tennis?' I said mildly.

'Or a croquet lawn. Not made my mind up yet,' he said, heading for the door set in the opposite wall. 'I'm not here often enough to make a proper garden of it.'

'So, where do you work?'

'We're based in the City,' he said. 'I'm in property development. Only get back here weekends.'

I glanced back at the gabled roof and tall chimneys of the house, above the high garden wall. Rather large for a weekend cottage, I thought. Doubtless it was a good investment.

'It's such bliss to get back here to true peace and quiet after a hectic week. This is a real treat for me, a long weekend. And it's great to see the horses again,' he added, rather wistfully I thought. 'There's something just so noble and reassuring about horses. Once they trust you, they're utterly dependable. No lies, no evasions. Just pure loyalty,' he said. 'Same with dogs, I suppose. So what's this little fellow's name?'

I glanced down at William sitting dutifully at my feet.

'Actually, he's not my dog,' I said.

'No?' There was that look in his eyes again, of amusement and suspicion in fairly equal measure.

'He's my neighbour's. He's called William. The dog, I mean, not the neighbour. She's Violet. I promised him a good walk. He's something of a hero.'

He paused to open the garden door for me, his glance intrigued.

'A hero, eh?'

I wasn't entirely sure I wanted to tell him everything about my encounter with Lee Brooks. I didn't want to sour the beauty and tranquility of the moment. The phrase 'fat bitch' jarred in my memory.

'An unwelcome guest at the cottage,' I said crisply. 'You said you'd found something to do with the Dash family?'

'Yes.' He hesitated, evidently still struggling to visualise William as a hero. 'But first I wanted to show you where we found it.'

Beyond the garden door was an oblong of garden, backed by clipped yew hedges. The wide gravel path was flanked by strips of bare earth planted with shrub roses, rather forlorn-looking, stiff as sentries in a well-spaced row, forever at attention. At the far end of the walk was a summer house.

'I was going to pull it down but Liddy insisted we restore it,' he said, pushing open the glazed door that squeaked on its ancient hinges. Inside, the air was stale and musty, the room gloomy from the trees that blocked out most of the sunlight. 'This is where we found it,' he said. He bent down and carefully lifted up one of the patterned cream and red tiles. 'They were loose and uneven. I'd asked the builder to relay them. There was a hollowed out space, and a small silver box buried. A pin box, I've been told. Must have lain there hidden for years. It's inscribed with the initials H.D.'

'Harriet Dash. Like the quilt,' I said excitedly. 'I wonder why she hid it in here?'

'Exactly what Liddy said.'

'You've still got the pin box then?'

He nodded. 'Liddy took a fancy to it. I'll show you. Come on, the coffee's probably ready now.'

'Oh, is Liddy here too?' I asked.

'Lord, no. She's not due back till the autumn.'

I hurried to keep up with him, huffing and puffing in the late morning sunshine. What kind of marriage was this when he and his wife spent the entire summer apart?

He stopped at the side door of the house and hauled off his boots in the porch, then padded across the tiled floor into the kitchen. The room was painted a warm cream, presumably to make up for being built on the shady side of the house. Pale sage cupboards flanked a huge cream Aga, the worktops a rich oiled beech. I wondered how the kitchen had looked when the Dash family lived here with their pageful of servants. I imagined the room full of steam from the pots and pans bubbling on the range, the cook and kitchen maid busy at the table, yelling at the scullery maid, producing mountains of pies and puddings to feed the family and the servants every day. Not a microwave or a ready meal in sight. Running the Hall must have been more like a small business than a family home. Now the immaculately ordered room bore scant hint of culinary activity except for the coffee pot on the table and a plate of what looked promisingly like home-baked ginger biscuits.

'Isn't she wonderful?' he beamed, pouring the coffee. 'Rhiannon comes in weekends to make sure I'm fed. She looks after the place a couple of mornings a week while I'm away. Keeps it shipshape.'

'She's certainly a good cook,' I said appreciatively through the crumbs.

'Farmer's daughter,' he said. 'She works at the Plough in Bishops Castle. I told her she should train and run her own restaurant. It'll be a good investment.'

On the wall next to the dresser I saw a board covered with photos. I recognised Gabriel grinning back from under ski hat and goggles, and in a wetsuit posing beside a surfboard. There were red and blue rosettes pinned round the board, and pictures of riders and show jumps. Mostly pictures of a beautiful young blonde girl. Too young to be the absent wife, I guessed. Had he a daughter then?

He saw me looking at the photos.

'That's Liddy,' he said with an unashamedly proud smile. 'One of the horse shows last year. She's totally fearless. Which I find terrifying,' he added with a rueful smile.

'Liddy?' I must have looked perplexed. I'd assumed 'Liddy' was the absent wife.

'My daughter, Lydia,' he said with a sparkle of curiosity in his eyes. 'She's away on a gap year at the moment.'

I wondered if he'd noticed my reaction: a reaction I could only describe as relief. There didn't seem to be a woman in his life. Not one that mattered as much as Lydia obviously did. He spoke of no-one else. Apart, of course, from the treasure that was Rhiannon. I hadn't needed to yell 'yippee'. My face betrayed exactly what I was thinking, and, as a property developer, Gabriel Haywood was skilled at assessing what people were thinking, predicting what was needed to clinch a deal. He wouldn't find my thoughts much of a challenge.

'She's very pretty,' I said.

'A beauty. Like her mother.'

I nodded. And though I desperately wanted to ask him outright where her mother was, I just knew I couldn't. That would be too obvious.

'More coffee?'

'You said you'd got the pin box?' I reminded him.

'So I have. It's up in Liddy's room. Won't be a moment. Help yourself to another biscuit,' he called back, retreating from the room.

I did. They were good.

There were more photos across the room, I noticed. Photos of his wife, I wondered?

I peered up at the picture of a tall slender young woman standing in front of a piano. Her long blonde hair hung over one shoulder, her dress a sleek column of black silk. Lydia was, indeed, a beauty. Beside her stood another girl, their arms entwined. She was holding a violin bow. I frowned and peered more closely. The girl's hair was short, curly, her wide lips smiling. I knew her. And I remembered exactly where I had seen her before.

'That was taken at the end of term last year. The Summer concert,' he said, coming back into the room. 'Lydia's a pianist. Lord knows where she gets that from! She got an A star in her Music 'A' level.'

I turned to him, feeling the room suddenly chill.

'The other girl in the picture … do you know her?' I said.

He gave a slight shrug. 'She's a friend of Liddy's. She came here once or twice. Nice girl.'

'It's Nicola Price,' I said, my stomach churning. 'They found her body yesterday morning, up at Bury Ditches.'

'Oh Lord,' he said, staring at me in anguish. 'I heard a girl had been murdered. I was just glad Liddy wasn't around. But Nicola … I never thought … they didn't give a name. You're sure?'

'The police came to interview me. I saw Nicky the day before in Ludlow. I was looking for Caitlin. You know, the girl with the quilt? She'd been staying with me, then she disappeared and I was worried about her. I didn't know where she'd gone. I saw Nicola in the market, and from the way she was dressed and made up, well, I thought at first she was Caitlin.'

He gave a shake of his head and sighed deeply.

'Bloody awful,' he said gruffly. He glanced up at me. 'Did you find her? Caitlin?'

142

I swallowed, my body tense. I was aware of my heartbeat hammering behind my ribs.

'No. Not yet,' I said, my mouth dry. 'I know she was here, Wednesday morning. I think she wanted to do some research into her family history.'

'She was here?' He shook his head. 'I wouldn't have seen her. I didn't get back from London till two. Not long before you turned up as a matter of fact.'

I clutched my hands together, aware I had been shaking. Now the nervousness began slowly to subside.

'What about Rhiannon? You said she's here a few mornings in the week. Could she have seen her? Spoken to her?'

'Not Wednesdays. She does a catering course,' he said.

I sighed. 'A friend of mine gave her a lift from Edgton up to Bury Ditches. After that, she just seems to have disappeared.'

'I take it the police know she's missing?'

'Yes, but I'm not sure how high a priority she is, now they're involved in a murder enquiry. They just seemed to think it wasn't unusual, a teenager taking off after a family row.'

'I'm sure there's nothing to worry about. Caitlin will turn up in her own good time,' he said, trying to sound reassuring. I nodded weakly, grateful that at least his calm air had not set alarm bells ringing. He even spoke Cat's name without the faintest tremor. Of course he was innocent of any involvement in Cat's disappearance, or worse, Nicky's death. He hadn't even been here on Wednesday morning. I summoned a smile.

'Look, this is the pin box I told you about,' he said. He set it down on the table. The silver was tarnished but the engraving was still legible. A swirl of initials. Was it really Harriet's? I held my breath. It was strange to

143

think I had been working on the quilt she had made. That the pins she had once used to piece the fabric had been taken from this little box. I opened the lid and peered in. The felt lining had all but disintegrated. There were a few rusty pins secured in a scrap of fabric. Beneath were fragile pieces of paper cut into hexagons.

I gave a little gasp.

'They're pattern pieces,' I told him. 'Harriet was using them to make the quilt.'

'Why don't you take it? You can give it to Caitlin when she gets back.'

'But I couldn't!'

'Why ever not? Liddy won't want it now. She's off to Oxford in the autumn. She'll have her mind on other things. Young men, mostly, I suppose' he sighed. 'Yes, keep it. It belongs with the quilt after all.

'Thanks,' I said warmly. 'I know Cat will be thrilled.' When she gets back. There had been no doubt in his tone. I had to believe in him. He wasn't even there the morning Cat had turned up at the Hall. I glanced down at William, happily crunching one of the biscuits Gabriel had sneaked to him. Trust your instincts, I told myself. 'So what's Lydia going to study?'

'English and Italian. She did well enough in her 'A' levels but she felt it would help to immerse herself a little more in the language. So as soon as she'd had her offer from Pembroke College, she went off to the Dolomites in January. I know some people who run a ski school in Val Gardena. Now she's in Tuscany, working in a hotel some friends of mine own.'

'She was at school here though? With Nicola?'

'At Beechwood, yes,' he said. 'Their music department is excellent. I told you Liddy's a pianist. They helped her tremendously, developing her

144

composition pieces. I did get some private tuition for her to make sure she got the grade she needed for Oxford. There's a very good teacher locally. Her son was at the same school actually. A very gifted musician. I think Ben's there in the photo you were looking at.'

'Ben? Ben Thomas is in the photo?'

He fetched the photo for me. I had been too focused on Lydia to notice him. Now I could see him, standing in the background at the other side of the piano: an earnest young man, tall and gangly in a dinner jacket and a bow tie that looked too big for his thin neck. Thick rimmed rectangular glasses under a long dark fringe. I saw something in his look, the intense, almost anxious way he was watching Lydia. Did Caitlin know, I wonder? She might have been Ben's best friend, but it was Lydia he was hopelessly in love with. The beautiful talented unattainable Lydia, two years his senior who probably never even acknowledged his existence. Lydia had been sitting her 'A' levels within weeks of Ben's death, yet still had gone on to shine with a starred A grade, her ticket to Oxford. I stared at the smiling self-possessed young woman. Had his death really meant so little to her?

Music: was that the connection, I wondered? The reason for Ben's suicide, for Nicky's murder, for Caitlin going missing? Was Beechwood at the heart of it all?

I took William back to Appletree Cottage and showed Vi the pin box. I told her about the photo of Lydia with a doting Ben in the background.

'Gave me quite a shock, seeing him there with the girls,' I told her. 'I've just got that niggly feeling, you know, that something's not right. Something about

Beechwood School maybe. Think about it. Ben was a music student, so was Nicky, and Cat's one of their art students. Two of them are dead and Cat's gone missing. There has to be a link.'

'Still no news about her then?' Vi asked.

I shook my head. 'Not that I've heard,' I said. 'I hate to think of her, out there somewhere on her own, with no money.'

'That's assuming she is on her own,' Vi said. 'You know what these young girls are like. Making unsavoury attachments their parents wouldn't approve of.'

'Thanks. That's very reassuring,' I told her. 'The police asked me what Cat had been doing on the computer. They mentioned Facebook. But the way she spoke that evening, the note she left me ... I'm sure she hadn't intended taking off. It had to be a spur of the moment thing, though what sparked it, I've no idea. I just feel sure she hadn't arranged to meet anyone.'

'Until we find her, we can't be sure of anything,' Vi said bleakly.

Back home I looked up Beechwood School's website. According to the list of staff, Dr Philip Mackay, a thin-faced smiling young man with ginger hair, was head of music. He must have known both Ben and Nicky well, and Lydia for that matter. Though there was no reason to think he could have any idea where Caitlin had gone, he might know a little of the 'why'. Anything that might help track her down had to be worth pursuing.

I parked on the gravel beside a school van. An elderly man in blue overalls was clipping the row of small box balls that rimmed the square of lawn like french knots in a tapestry. The large round clock on the wall chimed

146

four as I crossed the panelled hall of Beechwood School, following in the wake of a diminutive girl in neat navy and white uniform and plaits. The Music School was a swanky new building of glass and timber behind the main house. As I approached I could hear the scrape of a violin being played and the more lilting notes of a piano.

'Miss Jones, come in, come in,' the sandy haired man beckoned me, moving a pile of music manuscripts from the chair to the already laden desk. Dr Mackay's hair, I noticed, was somewhat sparser than appeared on his web photo, but he was wearing an identical spotted bow tie with his cord waistcoat. 'Not a prospective parent, I gather?'

'No,' I admitted. 'I'm a textile artist. It's Ben Thomas I wanted to ask you about. I met his mother recently.'

'Ah, yes, Ben,' he said, with a shake of his head. 'Do sit. A great shock to us all, I must say,' he told me, a faint Scots lilt to his voice. 'A sad loss to the school, and of course to his family.' He sat down beside me, crossed his legs, his long bony fingers looping round his knee. 'I'm sorry I can spare you but a few minutes. Practice, you know. We have a concert to rehearse. Lower fifth wind,' he confided. I stared at him, and fought very hard not to smile. 'You must understand, I can't discuss our pupils with you. I do have a duty of care and confidentiality.'

'I appreciate that,' I told him. 'I wouldn't have come if I didn't think it was vitally important. It's a matter of some urgency,' I said.

'Indeed?' His pale eyes blinked as if startled, behind his wire-framed glasses.

'A friend of Ben's came to see me a few days ago. Caitlin Brooks. She was a pupil here too.'

147

He gave a thin smile.

'Not one of our musicians,' he said.

'No. She's an artist.'

'Yes, I remember Caitlin,' he said, his lips pursed. 'Urban art.'

'The thing is, she told me she was leaving home, going to London. I thought I'd persuaded her to stay with me until she'd done her exams. But then, she disappeared. There's been no word from her. No-one seems to know where she is.'

He nodded. 'I can assure you it's a matter of some concern for us all,' he said. 'The Head had a visit from the police. Of course we wish we could help, but Caitlin is on study leave. But she did catch the school bus on Wednesday morning, though she never arrived here.'

'The school bus? You're sure?'

'The Head checked the log. The police were fully informed,' he said primly.

'So, what time was that?'

He sighed. 'It picks up about eight in Bishops Castle and does a circuit of some of the villages before reaching here at eight forty-five.'

'Does it go through Edgton?'

'Yes, I believe so,' he said tetchily. 'I don't keep the timetable personally. But we still have two pupils in the area.'

'She got off the bus at Edgton. Didn't the driver think it unusual?'

'Of course not. George said she told him she was on study leave. He just assumed she was going to study at a friend's house.'

'And then what? Didn't anyone see her?' I demanded.

'If we had, we would have informed the police,' he said. 'And I really don't see that Caitlin's whereabouts are any concern of yours, Miss Jones.'

'A girl has been murdered,' I reminded him angrily. 'And Caitlin is still missing.'

'Of course, with what's happened to Nicola, we are all very concerned,' he retorted. He gave a helpless shrug of his thin shoulders. 'It's quite appalling. It's normally a quiet and happy school, a hive of creativity and co-operation. And now this.' He threw up his hands. 'Where will it all end?'

'Nicola was a pupil of yours, wasn't she?'

'Indeed she was. She left last summer of course. She was taking a gap year. She had a place at Bristol University starting this autumn. I saw her only a few weeks ago, working in a local supermarket, stacking shelves to save up for her studies. A most promising pupil. Another tragic waste.'

'And both of them your pupils,' I said.

He winced. 'We all had such hopes for Ben. His was a rare gift.'

'No-one suspected he was troubled enough to take his own life?'

He straightened, his face flushing. Obviously he thought I was trying to blame him for what had happened.

'I mean, did he give any indication he was worried about his exams? About anything?' I said.

'There was an inquest,' he reminded me coldly. 'No blame was attached to the school. Indeed, our support for our pupils was judged exemplary.'

'I'm sure. All the same, Ben must have had something on his mind. Something that so troubled him, he took his own life.'

'You have to understand. Ben was not a communicative boy. At least, not verbally. Ah, but when he played,' he said more softly, his eyes closing, his body swaying slightly as if to some secret melody.

'He was two years younger than Nicola.'

'Yes. He was due to take his GCSEs last summer.'

'And Nicola was in the same year as Lydia Haywood?'

'Yes, yes. They were friends. Played in the same ensemble.'

'I gather Lydia's a talented pianist too.'

'Most accomplished,' he said, sitting suddenly upright again. His glance went to the bust of Beethoven perched on the shelf above his desk. 'Though I'm sure she won't mind me saying that her relationship with Euterpe was a little strained.'

'Euterpe?'

'The muse of music, Miss Jones,' he said solemnly. 'Lydia had to work hard on her composition. Inspiration did not come easily to her.'

'But she achieved an A star in music.'

'Oh yes. I did my best, of course, to draw out the talent in her. As did Ben.'

'She worked with Ben?'

'I know he was two years her junior, but his talent was precocious. He helped with several of our ensembles. He could be truly inspirational.'

I remembered the photograph. An anxious figure, shadowed in the background. A genius yet totally self-effacing. And, I suspected, totally besotted by Lydia Haywood.

'Judge for yourself,' he said. He got up and reached for one of the manuscript pads on top of the piano. He handed it to me. I saw the inscription on the front cover. '*Für Lydia.*'

'Ben's?'

He nodded. 'A piano sonata. Exquisite. Caitlin brought it to show me. She'd found it among Ben's things when they were clearing his room.'

'Caitlin?' I frowned. 'You mean, she was here? But, when? When did you see her?'

His cheeks coloured. He looked flustered. Guilty, almost. His glance swivelled to the calendar pinned on the wall. He got to his feet, peering at the calendar. 'I was due at rehearsal. She just turned up. Must have been last week. No, wait. There it is,' he said, his long forefinger stretched out, tracing the days. He turned back to me, triumphant. 'Monday morning. Just before first break.'

'And you didn't think to mention that to the police?'

'It wasn't relevant,' he insisted.

There was a light knock at the door. A boy appeared, clutching a briefcase in one hand, a flute in the other.

'Dr Mac?'

'Yes, yes, come, Daniel. I'm sorry, Miss Jones, but we must crack on. I'm sorry I can't be of more help to you.'

'Why did Caitlin bring the music to show you?'

He frowned, his hands flapped in agitation, as if seeking the keyboard to calm them.

'She was asking about Ben. Just as you are. Wanting to make sense of what had happened, I suppose. She wanted to know what I thought of the music. I glanced through it, and played a little for her. It had an elegiac quality, I thought. It was really remarkable. And quite beautiful. She left rather quickly then. As if she was in a hurry to be somewhere else.'

'She didn't say where she was going?'

He shook his head.

As I closed the door behind me, I could hear the first haunting notes of a flute. I remembered the photo in Gabriel Haywood's kitchen. I knew for certain now that Ben was hopelessly in love with Lydia. She was his muse, his inspiration for a sonata of exquisite beauty. Elegiac indeed, for it was probably the last thing he had played before he died. I recalled the anguish in the boy's eyes. The pain of unrequited love. Was it surprising that he had been besotted by Lydia? Even the scholarly Dr Mackay seemed not entirely immune from her spell. So how had Lydia treated the young man who had worked with her to improve her composition? Had she been kindly but remote, as if he were no more than a doting puppy following her around? Had she flattered him, turned on her charm, to persuade him to help her? His teacher had called him 'inspired'. Yet it was Lydia who had achieved the A star grade.

I just wished I had the talent to read the music Ben had written for her. Dr. Mackay was impressed. Did Mrs Thomas know just how talented Ben had been? And, as she had taught Lydia privately, she must have known the true extent of Lydia's talent. Had she gone to Cropstone Hall to teach the girl? Or had Lydia gone to her house at Henbatch? Was that the reason for Mrs Thomas's unease? Because she knew exactly how much help Ben had given Lydia to ensure she achieved the high grade she needed to secure her place at Oxford. But did Gabriel know too?

Poor Ben. How painful it must have been to work so close to Lydia, wanting to anything for her, totally in thrall to her. Such a sensitive and introspective young man had little other outlet other than his music. Little to shelter him from the storms of life and love. It wasn't hard to imagine just how devastated he had been when Lydia had finally abandoned him once he'd served his purpose. Hadn't that been the catalyst for his taking his own life?

Lost in thought, I realised I'd taken a wrong turn as I emerged from the Music School. I now found myself at the stables, with sleek plump ponies grazing in the paddock. I heard a bubbling laughter. In the yard two girls led out their grey ponies, ready saddled for a ride.

'Looking for me?' someone called.

I turned to see a tall, broad shouldered young man walking towards me. His short-sleeved T-shirt showed off the bulging muscles of his forearms. In tight jeans and riding boots, he had the kind of earthy good looks that I was certain must attract a loyal band of young admirers. I wasn't entirely immune myself.

'No, I've just been to see Dr Mackay,' I said with only the slightest of blushes.

'Well, if there's anything I can do for you that the doc can't, you let me know,' he said with a wink. He pushed open the gate. 'Caroline, how's Maisie's fetlock today?' he called, strolling into his domain. The girls looked round, faces shining, adoring.

'Keith, can you give me a leg up?'

With a simple, fluid movement, he caught the pony's bridle, seized the girl by the boot, and propelled her into the saddle. I half expected a round of applause.

As I drove back to my cottage, something niggled at the back of my mind. I pictured the girls busy grooming, wheeling barrows of dung, hauling hay. And thought of Gabriel, emerging from the tackroom in jodhpurs and riding boots.

'Horses!' I said out loud. Gabriel had told me he was away during the week. Rhiannon came in a few mornings to take care of the house. So who, I wondered, took care of the horses?

The lunchtime diners had all but finished as I waited at the bar of The Plough in the steep main street of Bishops Castle.

'Sorry. We've just finished the lunch orders,' the girl at the bar told me.

'That's OK. It was Rhiannon I wanted to speak to. Is she working here today?'

'She'll be off at three if you want to wait,' she said.

I waited, with a gin and tonic. I was just considering a second when a young woman in jeans and a T-shirt printed with The Plough's logo appeared at my table.

'Liz said you were asking for me?' Rhiannon said. She looked tired, her hair escaping in strands from her pulled back ponytail. I felt guilty for keeping her when I was sure she'd much rather be headed home for a break after a busy lunchtime service.

'I'm a friend of Mr. Haywood's,' I told her. 'I was over at Cropstone Hall today and he said you look after the house for him and do some cooking.'

'Just a few hours a week,' she said, suspicious. 'It's all legit. Tax and NI, the lot.'

'I'm sure. I've been trying to find someone. Caitlin Brooks. She was at Lydia's school. I think she went to the Hall on Wednesday morning. I hoped someone might have seen her there.'

She gave a shake of her head, and looked somewhat relieved.

'I do a catering course Wednesdays,' she said.

'You heard about the girl they found at Bury Ditches.'

'Course. That's not her, is it?' she said in alarm.

'No,' I said hastily. 'But it's made me worry all the more where Caitlin is. You didn't see her in Edgton then? She's sixteen, dresses as a Goth.'

154

'No. I'd have noticed, right?' she said wryly.

'Right,' I agreed.

'Sorry. I hope you find her,' she said warmly, her thin face easing with a smile. 'Doesn't make you feel safe, does it, when you know there's someone like that about.'

'There's one other thing,' I said as she turned away, conscious I was sounding like Columbo. She gave an impatient sigh and glanced at her watch.

'I've got to go,' she said. 'Got to pick up my kid, OK?'

'Sorry,' I said, resisting the urge to say she didn't look old enough to be a mum. Hardly more than a child herself. 'I just wondered about the horses,' I said, before she could escape. 'Mr Haywood's horses. Who takes care of them while he's away?'

'Well I certainly don't muck 'em out, dirty smelly brutes,' she said.

'Does someone come in from the village then?'

'No. Keith comes over and sees to them.'

'Keith,' I repeated. Where had I heard that name?

'Yeh, Keith Milford. He manages the stables at Beechwood School, gives riding lessons and I don't know what else,' she added with a throaty chuckle. 'See you later, Liz,' she called, sashaying out.

'Six thirty, remember. Don't be late. We're fully booked tonight.'

I stared after her. Keith Milford must have known Cat from school. Had he been at Cropstone on Wednesday morning when she was there? Had he spoken to Cat?

As I drove back up to my cottage, I went over the timing for Wednesday morning. Caitlin had left the cottage before eight and caught the school bus to Edgton. She must have gone straight to Cropstone Hall for she was back at the bus stop soon after nine, for Clive had picked her up there and taken her on to Bury Ditches. She was meeting someone, she'd told him. Was Keith my missing link, the 'someone' she'd arranged to meet, after he'd finished with Gabriel's horses? Had he picked her up at Bury Ditches and given her a lift somewhere?

In the studio I took out the little hexagons from the pin box Gabriel had given me. On one I recognised Harriet's handwriting. The words were faint but still legible.

'*Rambler was sick. I think I've found it.*' The second piece was in a different hand, perhaps cut from a letter. '*He said he'd make it known, about Jane.*'

Jane? Just who was Jane, and what did it have to do with Harriet Dash? I sighed, no closer to knowing what Harriet meant, and why she had gone to such lengths to conceal her thoughts within the quilt.

I spread her quilt out on the table again, studying the range of appliquéd and embroidered shapes of primroses and daisies, ferns, oak leaves, and holly. I knew from the scraps beneath that the pieces had some code to them, relating to what was written on the papers. But what did they mean? I added the script from the new pieces onto the list I had written out in a chart that paired them with the appliqué shape. Then, gathering up the list and the pin box, I went to see Vi.

'It's as if she's trying to tell a story,' I said, showing her the latest additions from the pin box. 'Only I don't understand what she's saying'.

Vi took the list from me, her small face pinched with a frown as she read, pausing now and again to study my sketches of the shapes Harriet had so painstakingly sewn.

'And these, the ones you found in the pin box – these must be the last ones she cut out,' she said at last.

'But she didn't use them,' I said.

'Perhaps she'd already finished the quilt and no longer needed them.'

'Then why hide them? It's as if she's ashamed of them.'

'Perhaps she meant to use them later and didn't have time.'

'Or she was afraid they'd be found.'

'Why not simply destroy them?'

'I don't know. Perhaps she still needed them for something. To remind her, perhaps, of all that had gone before. The quilt, everything. Sentimental reasons, maybe.'

Vi shook her head.

'It doesn't sound very sentimental to me,' she said. 'Did you find out what happened to the girl? Who she married?'

'No. There's no trace. Nor of her governess, Catherine Pendine. They can't simply have vanished.'

'Not having much success, are you,' Vi said with a gentle smile. 'I take it you're no closer to finding out where Caitlin went, either?'

I told her about my conversation with Rhiannon.

'I think the horse guy might have given her a lift somewhere. To the station perhaps. I'm hoping the police have managed to track her down on CCTV. But I know they have other priorities at the moment.'

'That dreadful business with Nicola.'

'I know. And to think her body was lying there, hidden in the undergrowth, the morning I was there. I never knew.' I gave a shiver. 'I saw the flowers Cat had left by the tree where Ben died.'

157

Vi glanced up at me from the pattern sketches. 'What flowers were they? Can you remember?'

'Just wild flowers. She must have picked them as she walked up from the car park. Why? Is it important?'

'Probably not,' she said. 'But seeing these pictures made me wonder. For the Victorians the language of flowers was very important, wasn't it?'

I nodded. 'I checked on some of them. Daisy for innocence, fern for sincerity, the red tulip for a declaration of love. I'm not sure it's the whole story though. I think our Harriet was a bit of an amateur botanist. The cuckoo pint doesn't seem to have any particular meaning – apart from being something of a phallic symbol, I suppose. It doesn't really seem very decorous for a young lady's quilt does it? And most of these berries are poisonous. I'm not sure exactly what message that's meant to convey. That leaf looks distinctly like white bryony, and that flower is definitely deadly nightshade. It all looks rather sinister.'

'Ah,' Vi said with a new sparkle in her eyes. She got up and went to her overstuffed bookshelves and prised out a dog-eared paperback. She handed it to me.

'L.P. Hartley,' she said. '*The Go-Between*. Charming story. Young Leo fancies himself a magician and endeavours to concoct a spell to dispose of the fiancé of the young woman he has a crush on. Belladonna for a beautiful woman. Atropa belladonna. Deadly nightshade.'

I stared at Vi.

'You think that's what Harriet is trying to do? Get rid of the governess she hates?'

'It's possible. After all, her father's widowed, perhaps he's looking to marry again, have more children. Of course the arrival of a beautiful young

158

governess will be a threat to her, and to her relationship with her father.'

'But to plot her murder … Is that why I can't find any trace of Catherine Pendine or Harriet after the 1881 census? Oh Lord, do you think she succeeded?'

'I think if there'd been a murder case, you'd have come across it by now,' Vi said, intending to reassure. I looked at her with less certainty. All manner of secrets could be buried at Cropstone Hall, I thought.

I was glad Caitlin wasn't there to share our discovery, and my suspicions. She was, after all, a descendant of Harriet's. It was an uncomfortable thought, having murder in the blood. A descendant. I smiled, relief returning to calm me.

'Of course she didn't succeed,' I said. 'Harriet must have married, mustn't she? Cat's her three times great-granddaughter.'

'She'll turn up, I'm sure of it,' Vi said.

'Caitlin?'

'And Harriet. With husband and family. They can't have disappeared, can they?'

'No. I'm not giving up yet,' I told her.

'What about your exhibition? Has Clive calmed down yet?'

I gave a rueful smile. 'Not yet, more's the pity, but there's nothing I can do.'

'Except find another venue,' Vi said sternly. 'You can't give up.'

'I know. I don't intend to. But I haven't even finished the quilts yet, what with all these distractions.'

'So tell me about your Gabriel.'

'He isn't 'my' Gabriel!' I protested. 'And I still don't know if he has a wife somewhere.'

'You mean you didn't ask him?' she said astonished.

'Perhaps I should take you with me next time. You can ask him,' I said.

Her glance was shrewd. 'So you're planning a next time?'

'No! I just meant ... well, I'm sure I'll bump into him again. He doesn't live that far away, after all. Not that it matters. I'm not looking for someone new.' I insisted, but I remembered how I'd felt when he'd told me Lydia was his daughter. I knew I wasn't being entirely honest. And Vi, from her look, suspected that too. 'OK, so I admit it. I was relieved to know Lydia wasn't his impossibly beautiful wife.'

'The lovely Lydia,' Vi said. She tucked L.P. Hartley back onto the shelf and returned with another book in her hand and held it out to me. 'You reminded me.'

I took the book from her and read the title: '*Love for Lydia.*'

'H.E. Bates. It's about a beautiful and imperious young woman who enjoys tormenting the young men who fall in love with her.'

'Like Ben?' I suggested. 'He wrote a piano sonata for her. The music teacher said he had outstanding talent. He was very shy, introverted. I suppose the music was his way of telling her what he felt about her.'

'But we don't know how she reacted. Not favourably, I imagine,' Vi said.

'All the same, young men don't kill themselves these days because the girl they adore doesn't want them. Do they?'

'No, but sometimes jealousy can drive people to extremes.'

I could feel myself blushing. Vi didn't know. How could she? I hadn't told anyone. It was hardly my finest

160

hour after all. An episode in my life that was now strictly off limits.

'Bron?'

'It's OK. Just thinking, that's all. Nothing important,' I said. I could see the shrewd gaze was not fooled. 'I'd better go. Loads to do if I'm ever going to get those quilts finished.'

I knew I was being a coward. But I had my reasons. I'd moved on, moved away. I didn't want to resurrect what I'd gone through when Ed left. I wasn't the same person. My quilts had saved me. Channelling my energy and passion into my work had let me breathe again. They'd given me back my life.

I worked late into the evening, determined to finish the autumn wall hanging, tacking together the layers, and feeding them under the sewing machine needle to quilt them together. As the coils and swirls of free stitching flowed, I tried to imagine just how desolate Ben Thomas must have felt when he decided to take his own life. And I thought of Caitlin, blissfully unaware of the depths of his feelings. Until a year later, and she had gone to help Ben's mother clear his room and had found the sonata. Until the moment Ben's tutor, Dr Mackay, had played some of the music for her. *Für Lydia*.

According to Dr Mackay, Cat had left in a hurry that Monday. But she was not running away. She had some mission in mind. I thought of Harriet, a century before, planning meticulously the removal of her rival. Plotting a murder in thread and patchwork. Had Cat inherited her deadly determination?

6

HARRIET

'Robert Meredith?' Catherine Pendine stared across the breakfast table, the colour drained from her face.

William Dash held out the letter he had received that morning, his glance stern upon Harriet's face.

She had returned from Hopwood Hall only a few days before, and the memory of Jane Pendine's face came back to her as she saw the change in her governess's expression. She stared coldly at her, reading the guilt plainly in her face.

'Mr Meredith is a friend of the Watkins family, Papa,' Harriet told him. 'He was kind enough to show me round the cathedral.'

'Don't you already have an understanding with Thomas?' he demanded.

'I am fond of Cousin Thomas, of course, but if Mr Meredith has fortune enough and a good name, perhaps he may be permitted to call?'

She was aware of the sudden clatter of a knife falling. Her quick glance at Catherine saw the icy glare in her eyes.

'He is not to be trusted,' she said hoarsely.

'Catherine, are you acquainted with this gentleman?'

The governess got to her feet, half stumbling, holding to the table as if to stop herself falling.

'No,' she said sharply. 'I have no acquaintance with him. It's only what I've heard. Gossip,' she said, breathless.

'What kind of gossip, Madam?' he demanded.

She gave Harriet a despairing glance, her face drained of colour. She turned to face her employer, her hands clenched together.

'I hear he has debts. Gambling debts. His estate at Radnor is a ruin. I think, before you approve his visit, you should enquire of Mr Adcott if he considers Robert Meredith a fit companion for your daughter, Sir. Please excuse me.'

Lily of the Valley, laburnum, the deadly hemlock with its parsley-like leaves and purple-blotched stems: what infinite variety of poisons there were at hand, Harriet thought. She retreated to her room to change into her outdoor skirt, convinced she had to do something soon. Now she had seen Jane Pendine, and was aware of the woman's precarious situation, she knew just how desperate Catherine was to secure her father's fortune for herself. What would she do then? Bring her sister here, to Cropstone Hall, as companion perhaps?

'And where's my place in her plans?' Harriet thought angrily. Married off, doubtless, to a buffoon like Thomas Watkins. Demurely trotting round the farms and cottages in Mrs Watkins' wake, dispensing charity.

And what of Robert Meredith? She touched her throat, her neck, shadowing her memory of his fingertips. She recalled, with a guilty blush, the heat and press of his body against hers, the taste of his lips. But what if the governess was right, and he had no fortune? What if he had misled her? Or had Catherine her own reasons for wanting Meredith kept away? Was she simply jealous? Once safely married and installed as mistress of Cropstone Hall, did she mean to renew her acquaintance with him? His lack of fortune would be no bar to their liaison then, for she would have a fortune of her own.

'My father's fortune,' she said bitterly. 'She will not take him from me.'

In the solitude of the summerhouse, she took out the piece of bacon she had concealed in her pocket at breakfast and wrapped within it a few seeds from a laburnum pod. While her father was occupied in his library, the dogs were dozing in the sunshine out of doors. It was a matter of moments before one of them was enticed to eat the bacon. Harriet walked back along the Rose Walk. The gardeners had been busy clipping the cherry laurel hedges. According to her book, the leaves could be distilled to make prussic acid, though the distinct bitter almond smell of cherry laurel water could be a bar to the governess drinking it. Could she disguise it in a glass of Madeira perhaps?

She shook her head. She could not risk failure. Yet she had need of something swift acting. There must be no mistake. Her pace quickened. She recalled exactly where in the hedgerow she had seen the bell-shaped purple-brown flowers of Atropa belladonna. Though it as yet lacked the shiny black berries, still the plant contained poison enough to kill: a plant described by John Gerard, the 16th century herbalist, as 'furious and deadly'. Harriet smiled as she recalled reading his words, and felt in her heart a strong affinity with the plant. Furious and deadly indeed. With gloved hands and small scissors, she clipped a spray of deadly nightshade and hurried back to the house.

On the lawn, one of the dogs, Rambler, was vomiting. The laburnum peas had been effective, but how much more potent was the flower she carried. She was certain now she had the answer.

Catherine Pendine was in conversation with her father in the library for some little while. Harriet took the nightshade to her room and carefully chopped up the leaves and stems with her scissors, and left the shreds soaking in a little warm water which she hoped to infuse with their poison.

When she returned to the drawing room, her father had gone.

'He's going to Ludlow to see Lawyer Adcott,' Miss Pendine informed her. 'On a matter of great urgency, he said.'

Harriet guessed the subject of his visit. And from Miss Pendine's taut smile, Harriet knew exactly who had poisoned her father's mind against Meredith.

'You look pale, Miss Pendine. I hope you are not troubled with stomach cramps again?' she asked. 'Mrs Watkins recommended ginger and warm milk. Might I ask Cook to prepare some for you?'

'It's kind of you, but no,' Catherine said. 'It's simply a headache. Perhaps I'll go and rest a little. We can practise your piano pieces later.'

Harriet drew out her sewing, convinced she now had the perfect opportunity. The spice of ginger in a warm drink would disguise all manner of strange flavours, wouldn't it?

She took up her sewing and embroidered a single red tulip, as a declaration of her love for Robert Meredith, and beside it a palm leaf for victory. Very soon she would have achieved both her goals: Catherine Pendine would be gone, and her betrothal to Thomas Watkins would be no more. Once her father returned, assured of Meredith's status, he would surely approve her choice.

She selected a length of pink silk thread and satin-stitched the petals of a sweet pea, with a curling chain stitch frond. The sweet pea was a symbol of farewell. That done, she rose and went to stir and drain the deadly nightshade liquid. She had just the thing to conceal it in: a small perfume bottle that had belonged to her mother. It would be easy to hide it in her pocket till the chance arose to add it to Miss Pendine's warm milk.

William Dash returned in time for dinner but in no mood to discuss his business in Ludlow with Adcott. The governess was still absent in her room, her headache not improved. Harriet dressed for bed, and began to write up her notes in her book of poisons. The little bottle stood ready on the dressing table.

There came a soft knock at her door, then she heard the governess's voice.

'Harriet, may I speak with you?'

Harriet glanced anxiously at the perfume bottle. It looked innocent enough. She hurriedly slid her note book under her pillow and went to the door.

'Miss Pendine, is something the matter? Shall I fetch some warm milk for you?'

The governess gave a sigh, plying her hands together. She looked anxiously into Harriet's face.

'Thank you for your kindness, but it is nothing physical that ails me,' she said. 'It troubles me that if I say nothing, you will be led into harm's way.'

She took a faltering step into the room, closing the door behind her. Her gaze cast about the room, as if still she debated within herself whether to stay and speak, or to flee at once. Again Harriet glanced anxiously to where the perfume bottle stood by her silver-backed brushes, her heartbeat drumming as if it were she who

166

had drunk of the poison brew.

'Your father has done me a great honour in asking me to be his wife. You should know, I have not as yet given him my answer.'

Harriet glared at her, arms folded. Had she come to ask her approval? What did she expect?

'You cannot take my mother's place,' Harriet answered coldly.

'I know that. I know my faults well enough,' she said in a low voice. 'And I am conscious of my duty to him, and to you, Harriet. It is my fault that you have been distracted from your own sense of duty by the attentions of this man.'

'You mean Robert Meredith?' Harriet said. In saying his name aloud she felt a new strength, certain of his love and of her affection for him. A single red tulip was not declaration enough. She should have filled a whole room with them. Her eyes blazed as she thought of him, the heat rising in her face.

'I told your father we were not acquainted,' the governess said, her head bowed.

'But you are, aren't you? You know him very well, I think.' As she glared at the woman, she saw the governess grow pale, tears standing in her eyes.

Was this the purpose of her visit: to warn her away from Meredith, and steer her to her proper course of marrying Thomas Watkins? That would leave her free to pursue Meredith herself.

'Has he spoken of me?' Catherine demanded.

How jealous she sounded, Harriet thought. She shook her head. 'Why would he? What do you mean to him?'

'Nothing,' she said bitterly. 'More's the pity.'

'You love him?'

'No!' she said in alarm. 'You are quite mistaken. My interest in him comes from another cause. A dreadful business: one that ensnares me and brings me shame.' Again she sighed and bowed her head. Slowly she sank down into the chair. 'I tried to protect you. I warned him to keep away from you.'

'You went to see him in Ludlow,' Harriet said.

'He's taken rooms there. Hiding from his debtors. Oh be assured, Lawyer Adcott will inform your father soon enough of the parlous state of Meredith's finances. But he doesn't know the depths of this man's evil.'

'Evil?' Harriet stared at her, the colour high in her cheeks. 'What has he done to hurt you so?'

'Not me. My sister, Jane,' she told her. When she looked up, Harriet saw the pain in her eyes. Her heart beat with a new alarm. She remembered Jane Pendine's pale anxious face. Like a ghost, her beauty all but dissipated. And the fear that dwelt so close beneath her placid surface.

'She fell in love with him?'

'Yes,' she said in a sighing breath. 'She believed in his sweet words. He pursued her relentlessly, but for sport, not love. And when he found other, richer quarry, he abandoned her and chased after them instead.'

'He broke her heart.'

'And her spirit too,' Catherine said. She reached out and took Harriet's hands into her own. 'You cannot trust him, Harriet. He will deceive and betray you too.'

'He was most attentive,' she said uncertainly. 'I confess I found his company agreeable. I thought I loved him,' she faltered.

'This is all my fault,' Catherine said in anguish. 'If I had not come here as your governess, he would not have found you. I was glad to think you would make your home with your cousin Thomas for at least you would be protected, close to those who truly love and care for you. I thought you were safe. Until now. You must promise me, you will not see him or speak to him again. You are in great peril.'

'If what you say is true,' Harriet began.

'Do not doubt it,' Catherine warned her. 'Robert Meredith wants only your fortune. And when he has what he wants, he'll squander it and leave you nothing.'

Harriet felt the sting of tears at her eyes. She thought of Meredith's gentle words, recalled his touch, his kiss. She pressed her eyelids tightly shut.

'But he loves me,' she insisted. 'And I do love him.' She dropped to her knees before her governess, her eyes imploring some way of finding happiness with Robert Meredith. She could not turn away from the one man she believed would bring her happiness.

'Then I have no choice,' Catherine said bleakly. She put her arm around the girl's shoulder and drew her close. 'You must listen to me, Harriet. What happened to my sister must not happen to you.'

How could she have been so foolish? Her stomach clenched with pain as if from a poison draught as she realised, appalled, how close she had come to succeeding in her plan. What would have happened to Jane without her sister's help and support? Desperately, angrily, Harriet threw the little bottle to the floor and crushed it with the fire irons until only splinters remained.

As the darkness beyond her window began to pale, and the birds began their raucous chorus, she pulled a grey velvet pelisse over her nightdress. Taking her poison notebook from its hiding place beneath her pillow, and the scissors she had used to harvest the leaves and flowers for her poisons, she wrapped them in a strip of silk from her patchwork fabrics, and softly made her way down over the stairs and out into the garden, while her father still slept and the servants were just rising to set the house upon its daily course.

She had to hide the evidence of her guilt. But where? The gardeners would notice soon enough if she tried to bury the package amongst the borders.

The gabble of ducks made her turn. Across the park, she saw the faint mist that hung over the still water of the lake. She walked quickly now, the light growing as the sun rose above the rim of hills. She glanced fearfully back at the house. At any moment someone from the house might see her and come after her.

The morning chill numbed her, the dew seeping up into the hem of her nightdress. The thin cotton dragged against her legs with the weight of water. She reached the grass bridge and halted, staring down into the lake. With a stone to weight it, her bundle would be lost in the mud at the bottom. But what if it floated back to the surface? And as she gazed down, uncertain, it was not her own reflection she saw, but the small oval face of Jane Pendine. How much had it cost her governess to tell her the truth of Meredith's perfidy?

Clutching the bundle, she crossed the bridge and walked a little way into the woodland beyond, where lately she had gathered cuckoo pint and bryony for her potions. On the far bank of the lake she stopped, and, stooping down, scrabbled with her fingernails and the scissor blades, to gouge away the layers of bracken, leaves and moss, and dig out a narrow hollow. There she placed the notebook and raked back the earth to cover it. She glared down at the mounded earth. In time it would rot into nothing, undiscovered. Catherine Pendine had nothing to fear from her now. She knew exactly what it was that the governess feared.

'Harriet, is it really you? Dear Lord, I prayed I might find you!'

She heard his voice like a dagger through her. She dusted off her hands, and slowly turned to confront him, aware even now of the melody in his voice that enchanted her, willing her to believe that Catherine had lied, that she could defy the world and go to him.

'What do you want?' she said, fearful.

'Lawyer Adcott told me I must never see you or speak with you again,' he said. 'I had to know if it was your wish, or theirs.'

Her glance flickered over him in alarm at his disarray. He looked careworn, unshaven, as if he too had not slept.

'Miss Pendine has told me about her sister.'

'Her sister?' He frowned, took a step closer to her. 'What has this to do with us?'

'You've forgotten so soon?' Harriet said bitterly. Briefly her gaze took in the line of his brow, his dark eyes, his lips that until so recently had seemed such temptation.

'No. Not forgotten,' he said in a low groan. 'But what could I do? I am pursued by debtors. At least she is safe. Cared for. And me, what harbour do I have?'

'Marriage, perhaps, to someone young and foolish and possessed of a fortune?' she said with an icy calm she did not feel.

His lips curled in a thin humourless smile.

'I own, it would have solved a great many problems. But I love you, Harriet. My feelings are no sham.'

'No? But they are most convenient, aren't they?'

'Do you blame me for wanting to make you my wife?' he pleaded. 'What chance did I ever have? My

171

life was ruined before ever I inherited my father's debts. Yet with you, I believe there's a chance after all for me ... for us both to find happiness. You can make me a better man, Harriet. I came here in the hope of getting a message to you. To beg you to speak with me one last time before I go. Now I see how foolish a hope that was.'

'You're going away?'

'I have no other choice. William Watkins did me a great favour by dying. My debts died with him, but there are others who aren't so obliging,' he said, his thin smile quite without warmth.

'Then I'm sorry for you. But I cannot help you.'

'But you can! There's still time,' he said urgently. 'That's why I had to come. Don't you see? I've thought of nothing else since I first saw you. Your sweet smile, your gentle voice, your touch.' He had drawn closer to her. So close he could have reached for her hand. She stood resolutely before him, chin tilted up, refusing to believe in the love he professed. How could she ever believe a word he said?

'And Jane Pendine,' she said, 'Do you never think of her?'

'She was just a governess, Harriet. Yes, I had some affection for her, but it was she who was besotted with me!'

'Then why did you pursue her?'

'I didn't, I swear. I told her, her dreams of marriage to me could never be. She had no money. I could give her nothing.'

'She bore your child!'

A look of anguish tensed in his face. Had he truly not known?

He frowned, his hands opening to her in supplication. 'You're right. Poor Jane needs my

172

support. But you see me before you, penniless, without help. What have I to offer her?'

'A name for her child,' she said coldly. 'Go now, before we are seen. Have no doubt, my father will not treat you kindly.'

'Harriet, please. Say you'll come away with me now. Why not? You love me, don't you? Your kiss did not lie.'

With an angry look, she turned from him.

'Just go.'

He came after her, caught her arm.

'Do I really mean so little to you? Have you no pity?'

'You mean nothing to me now,' she told him. 'Let me go.'

She tried to shrug away from him, but felt his grip tighten. A dark anger gleamed in his eyes as he stared at her.

'Then I will go. But not before I take what was promised,' he whispered hoarsely. He pulled her to him, his lips fastening on her mouth with a sudden fierce passion that took her breath from her. She struggled against him, but his body closed all the harder against her.

'Jane was no willing lover either,' he panted. 'But that didn't spoil my pleasure in taking her. On the contrary,' he said, dragging the cloak from her shoulders, his hands groping for her breasts beneath the flimsy fabric of her nightgown. 'This is one farewell I shall savour for a long time. Sweet Harriet. You and I shall be joined after all. As man … and wife.'

'No!' she cried out, helpless, as he pushed her to the ground and fell upon her, pressing his knees between her thighs. The rough skin of his cheeks rasped at her flesh as he struggled to hold her while he unbuttoned his breeches. Gasping for breath, her fingers tightened. Felt the cold metal of the scissors she had dropped. Fumbling, she grabbed at the scissors and stabbed the blade down hard into his shoulder.

He let out a cry, jolting back from her in pain, blood seeping, dripping onto her. It was no more than a few seconds, but enough for her to kick at him and roll free. Stumbling, she ran towards the lake and threw herself into the water as he came after her.

She felt the water close above her, its cold embrace dragging her down. Her limbs thrashed against the numbness. Her lungs ached. Then as her gown and cloak billowed up around her like the blowsy petals of a full-blown rose, she saw sunlight dappling through the murky green. Dimly she was aware of bubbles of sound from far off, then came a painful gasp of breath and water, before all grew still and calm and cold.

A woman's face seemed to float above her. Her mother's? She frowned. No. She knew that face. She had seen it once before, pale as a ghost, so fearful. And here she was again, bending closer. But there was warmth now. She could feel warmth through her body, and a scent of roses. Her eyelids flickered open.

'Harriet, you're all right … you're going to be all right.' There was joy in that voice, a melody she remembered. Her governess's voice. Catherine Pendine. And then the memories came flooding back. Of a man's eyes, dark with lust, of blood, and water.

'He was here,' she whispered. 'He came here for me.'

'No. It was a dream. Hush. Sleep now. You mustn't trouble yourself with dreams.'

'It was no dream.' Harriet's eyes opened wide. She recognised her bedroom, the curtains half drawn, the sunlight. She caught at the governess's wrist and drew her closer. 'Meredith found me. He'd been waiting, up in the woods,' she whispered, seeing Catherine Pendine's eyes widen in alarm at her words. 'He told me what he did to Jane. He said it was against her will. He tried to defile me too.'

She heard the woman's low curse. Then saw her nod.

'He's gone now. You're safe. A dream it was, after all,' she whispered, stroking her hair, tucking the sheets close around her. 'Sleepwalking. That's what the doctor told your Papa. A few weeks' rest and quiet, and you'll be fine again. Just sleepwalking,' she said, drawing away. 'I'll go and tell your father you're awake.'

The July afternoon was warm and scented from the lavender that bordered the lawn. Bees droned amongst the blossom. Under the parasol shade, Harriet sat with her embroidery. The quilt top was almost finished now. She patiently stitched her initials into one corner, together with the year. With each stitch she locked away the memories of the past few months: her mistrust of Catherine Pendine, her folly in believing in Meredith, her attempts to be rid of the governess for good. The memories shamed her, but she could not destroy the quilt. It was a fitting reminder of her foolishness, a warning to her that disgrace had not been far. And that, had she not been so wilful, she might now be mistress of Hopwood Hall, and wife to Thomas Watkins.

The shock of her near drowning had been hard for her father to accept, it seemed. Thomas Watkins had sent his wishes for her recovery, but the suspicions and doubts around what had happened to her had ensured his offer of marriage had not been forthcoming. His mother no doubt had been insistent on that. Who would marry her now, with that taint of madness about her? The humiliation of what had happened hung like a foul miasma about the house, and William Dash sought every opportunity to evade it. When he was not away on business or out riding, he spent most of his time in his library. Harriet rarely saw him. They lived separately within the vast spaces of the house like two planets in distant orbits. Harriet wondered if he would have preferred that she had died that day.

She read again the letter Catherine Pendine had left for her, though by now she knew it by heart. With Harriet safely restored to health, Catherine had left for France with her sister, to make a new life, safe from Meredith's reach.

'Do not judge a man by what he says, but by what he does,' she had written. *'Your father has always behaved with impeccable courtesy and kindness towards me. Though I was greatly honoured by his offer of marriage, I could not in all conscience accept.'*

In her letter, Catherine told her how Jane Pendine had been pursued relentlessly by Meredith, until at last he had forced himself on her. In time, she realised she was with child. He had refused to accept the child was his, so Jane had to leave her post and went abroad, taking a room in Dinard, a town she knew from her time as an English teacher there. As soon as she received Jane's letter, Catherine had left Hereford and gone after her, staying with her until her confinement in March. She had taken the child to a convent in the town and left her there in the care of the nuns, with what little money they could afford. As soon as Jane was strong enough, they had returned to England and Catherine had found a refuge for her at Belmont House. Though Jane's mind had been unbalanced by her ordeal, her place at the charitable home relied on her silence. Any hint of a scandal, of a child born out of wedlock, and she would be dismissed. Of course Meredith continued to deny any responsibility, and had no money to help pay for her keep, but he would always be a threat to them. *'He said he'd make it known, about Jane and her child and my part in concealing the birth. I knew he would, if it suited him. What had he to lose? So I agreed to sign over the small income I have from my late parents' trust fund. Lawyer Adcott arranged it though I could never tell him of Meredith's true part in Jane's history. Only that I was obliged to Meredith for his help in rescuing my sister from her difficulties in France. How that lie hurt me. Yet I had to do it. I bought his silence to keep Jane safe,'* Catherine confided. *'Money is the only thing he truly loves.'*

Harriet took up her scissors and carefully, deliberately, cut through the paper again and again until nothing remained of it but shreds, and one final hexagon, which she slipped for safety into her pin box with the last remnant of her diary.

'You look a picture of health, I must say,' Gwen said as Annie announced her visitor. 'No more sleepwalking, I hope?'

'No,' Harriet assured her with a faint smile.

'I thought I'd come and tell you my good news in person. And reassure myself that you are quite recovered.'

'What news?'

'That I'm to be married. At the end of August.'

'Oh Gwen, I'm so pleased for you! So, who is he?'

'James works for the railway. He's a porter at the station in Ludlow, and very fine he looks in his uniform too. He's got a promotion to Shrewsbury. And there's a cottage that comes with the job. We'll be making our home there in September.'

'You're moving away?'

Gwen's smile faltered at seeing the girl's regret.

'It really isn't so far. Just a few more stops on the train. If you've a mind, you'll be very welcome to visit.'

'Oh, Gwen …' She hung her arms around her former nanny's neck and hugged her. 'Of course I'm pleased for you. And I've a gift for you. See, it's almost finished.' She held up the quilt top for her to see. 'I've just to bind the edges and you shall have it in time for your wedding.'

'It's beautiful. And those fabric pieces, I remember them from your dear mama,' she said. 'I'll treasure it, truly, my dear, and remember all the happy times we had here together.'

It was finished at last. Harriet cut the thread and gazed down at the daisy she had embroidered, a token of loyal love and of simplicity. It was perfect for Gwen's wedding gift. The rose leaf design was the final shape on her patchwork: a symbol of hope for love. She felt guilty at having deceived Gwen into taking part in her plot against Catherine, using her name to seek information about the governess's past. Had the truth come to light, it could have cost Gwen her position, her reputation, and what would have happened to her then? Who would have believed in her innocence?

She folded the quilt top and set it down on the table and closed her sewing box. She got to her feet and slowly made her way through the garden, along the Rose Walk to the summerhouse, the little silver pin box in her hand, the last two paper hexagons hidden within: a scrap from Catherine's letter, and the last cut from the page of her diary.

She was glad Gwen would have the quilt. She had no need of it to remind her of her folly. How could she ever forget what her infatuation with Meredith had almost brought her to. But seeing the quilt gave her no rest, no chance to pick up the pieces to form a new life. It would always be weighted with memories, fastened into every stitch. Why wasn't life as easy to arrange and piece together as a quilt?

In the summerhouse, she pulled up the loose tile from the corner by the chair, and burrowed into the soft sandy earth with her fingers. She pressed the pin box into its hiding place and covered it over with the tile. Catherine's secret was safe now, as was her own.

She closed the door behind her and stood for a moment to gaze along the garden borders, determined to admire the beauty of the roses. Would she ever truly be free to enjoy the scents and colours of the garden again? The memories would always haunt her. She had no use for paints or embroidery now. Nothing that could remind her of that appalling day. What hope was left her now of happiness or love? What a mess she had made of everything. She was resolved to lead a more useful life, following Mrs Watkins' example by immersing herself in charitable work. She had need of redemption.

As she crossed the lawn to take her afternoon tea, she saw Annie bring another visitor to see her.

'I c-came to see your father. He said I might speak with you,' Samuel Kendall said. Harriet smiled in welcome and exchanged a somewhat puzzled look with the maid.

'Annie, would you fetch another cup for Mr Kendall,' she said. 'Mr Kendall, do take a seat.'

He studied her for a moment, twisting his hat in his hands.

'I … I understand you've no recollection of … that morning,' he began.

'Very little,' she said crisply. 'They say I was sleepwalking.'

She could feel her face begin to heat under his steady curious gaze.

'They didn't tell you…' he said, pausing to swallow, as if he were struggling with a particularly gristly mouthful. 'I … was the one who found you.'

'You?' She stared at him. Saw the confusion again in his eyes. Now he was beginning to blush too.

'I had come to the house immediately we'd had news that … a certain gentleman had quit his lodgings and disappeared. Escaping his debtors. Mr Adcott wanted to warn your father at once.' Another gulp. This time he glanced away across the garden, to the border of roses, the falling petals scattered over the lawn. 'I saw something in the lake. I ran … and saw you there half drowned. I … pulled you out of the water.'

'Oh. I see.' There was no look between them now, but each was transfixed by a vision of the other. Her hands curled, trembling, together. She had been dressed only in her nightshift that morning. Samuel Kendall had touched her, held her, carried her from the water. How intimately acquainted he was with her body. She bowed her head. And how much more closely acquainted was Meredith. She looked up and held her gaze levelly upon him. 'Then I owe you my life, Mr Kendall. I am most grateful.'

His blushes deepened.

'It isn't your gratitude I came for, Miss Dash, though that's most welcome, I'm sure,' he said. 'I wanted to let you know. Your father has given me a most generous reward. I've booked my passage to New

York. I'm giving up my old life here and going to make my way in America.'

'You're leaving us too,' she said with unfeigned regret. He looked at her in question. 'Miss Pendine has left for France with her sister. And my old nanny, Gwen, was here this morning to tell me she's to be married. She's going to live in Shrewsbury.'

'I wish her happiness,' he said warmly. 'I hope one day I too might find someone to share my life with.' His glance stole back to her face. 'It's difficult to continue living here I should not wish to embarrass you in the future by … memories of what happened,' he finished.

'That's most understanding of you,' Harriet said, though she felt there was more he was not saying. 'Thank you. And of course I wish you well in your new life. I envy you, starting afresh. As if the past had never been,' she said, her smile wavering. Resolutely she pinched her fingernails into her palm to stop herself crying. What purpose did self-pity serve? She deserved to be shunned, after all she had done.

'I won't forget everything about my past life here,' he said. He glanced at her and his glance did not dip away as it met hers. 'I told you once, I was your servant. I shall always be.' Awkwardly he got to his feet, almost colliding with Annie who was returning with the tea tray. 'Please excuse me. I really must go.'

'Mr Kendall, I should like to give you some small token of my thanks,' Harriet said quickly. She took the silver thimble from her sewing box and held it out to him. 'It was my mother's. It means a great deal to me.'

He took it carefully from her with a nod of thanks and, slipping it into his pocket, turned and strode away from her across the lawn.

'Shall I pour the tea, Miss Harriet?'

Harriet did not answer. Her gaze fell on the quilt. A daisy. For simplicity and loyal love. The rose leaf for hope. She thought of Catherine Pendine's letter.

'A new life. Can you imagine?' she said softly.

'Miss Harriet?'

She smiled up at the maid.

'No, Annie, I'll pour my own tea, thank you. In a moment.'

She laid back her head against the cushion of the chair and closed her eyes.

'*Money is the only thing he truly loves*,' Catherine had written in her letter.

'He said he loved me,' Harriet thought, and knew it was a lie. But where was Meredith now? Had he really gone? What if he came back there, to stand again in the shadow of the trees and wait for her? She gave a shiver. But there was something else in Catherine's letter that stirred her from the darkness of her thoughts. She remembered the cold water closing over her face. And then sunlight through the water, a dazzle that surrounded her, and a face, like a halo, above her, calling her name, tears falling.

'Harriet ... my darling Harriet ...'

She frowned. What was it Catherine had said? '*Judge a man by what he does...*'

She sprang up from her chair, and gathering up her skirts, set off across the lawn at a run. Round the corner of the house she caught sight of the trap heading down the drive, the chestnut horse striding out at a brisk trot. She called out, and started running again, faster this time, her heart pounding, her chest tightening so she could hardly breathe.

'Mr Kendall, wait! Oh please wait!' she cried out.

As the trap reached the high wrought iron gates, the carter slowed to turn into the lane. At that moment

Samuel Kendall looked back and caught sight of her. He called to the driver to halt, then jumped down onto the gravel as she caught up with them.

'Miss Dash, is everything all right?'

'Yes,' she said, breathless, her cheeks scarlet. 'I think perhaps it is.' She held out the rose leaf to him, her hand trembling. 'Will you write to me, Mr Kendall, as soon as you are settled in New York? I've a mind to travel. I should very much like to see what you make of your new life.'

BRON

Saturday morning

It was barely eight o'clock, but I couldn't risk waiting too long to find out. I rang Mrs Thomas's number.

'It's Bronwen Jones again, Mrs Thomas. Do you have a phone number for Caitlin's parents? Or their address?'

'I've got their address somewhere,' she said. 'Why? Have you found her? Is there any news?'

'No, I've heard nothing from her, I'm afraid,' I said. 'There was just something I needed to ask them that might help me find her.'

'I had a call from Dr Mackay,' she said. 'He told me you'd been asking about Ben.'

'It was Caitlin I was trying to trace,' I explained. 'He showed me the piece Ben had written for Lydia. He said it was outstanding. Did you hear him play it at home?'

'Bits and pieces,' she said. 'He was always working on it.'

'You didn't want to keep the manuscript?'

'No,' she said softly.

'May I ask why?'

She didn't answer at first. I heard her sigh. 'I think perhaps you already know why.'

Because of Lydia, I realised. She knew her son had been besotted by her. 'I can understand how you feel.'

'Can you?' she said bitterly. 'I very much doubt that.' She hung up. I felt guilty at having upset her again, yet I had to track Caitlin down. It was now more important than ever.

As I turned out of the lane, heading for the Brooks' house in Lydbury North, I passed a motorcyclist. For a moment I thought it was Lee Brooks. Though I was in no mood to face him again, it might have saved me a journey. I wondered if he'd even answer the door to me when I called there.

'I'm Bronwen Jones,' I told the woman at the door.

'You! You've got a bloody nerve coming here!' she said, her face pink with fury.

'I'm sorry. I'm just worried about Caitlin. It's been three days now. Have the police found any sign of her?'

'They've got her on CCTV,' she said. 'She caught the London train Wednesday afternoon,' she said fiercely. 'Not that it's any of your business!'

'And since then, have they any more news?'

'Not yet,' she said crisply.

It was something though. Relief that she wasn't lying dead on a hillside somewhere. Whoever had killed Nicky had not got Caitlin too.

'Your husband was right,' I said as she made to close the door. 'Cat brought the quilt to me but I'd no right to keep it. Here, I've brought it back,' I said, holding up the carrier bag.

'Damn right!' she said, snatching the bag from me. She peered inside to make sure I wasn't lying.

I swallowed. It was now or never. 'Mrs Brooks, might I come in for a few minutes? There's something I need to ask you.'

The smart detached house in a modern cul-de-sac on the edge of Lydbury North had been extended to double its original width. On the pristine gravel drive stood a new BMW. No sign of a motorbike, I'd noticed

185

with relief as I'd approached the front door. Inside, the large kitchen diner was immaculately fitted with dove grey units and gleaming stainless steel, the slate floor leading into a wide mock Victorian conservatory. The glossy décor was at odds with Cat's dystopian drawings and the impression she had given me of a home that was ramshackle and dysfunctional. I began to wonder about the tale she had told me of wrestling with her mother over the quilt, desperate to retrieve the money hidden inside. Was I wrong to believe what Cat had told me? And what of Lee Brooks? Was he really a posturing bully, or a caring stepfather driven frantic by worry? In the hall I'd noticed a large photograph of a beaming bride and groom. Taken just a few years ago, I guessed. I wondered if Caitlin had been as happy with her mother's remarriage.

Mrs Brooks made no move to switch off the large plasma screen TV that hung on one wall of the kitchen. She sat down in a wicker armchair in the conservatory. It was barely nine o'clock, but there was no sign of breakfast being made, and she was already smartly dressed in designer jeans and a beaded top. Evidently the Brooks were early risers.

'She stayed the night with you, didn't she?' she asked me.

'Yes. She said she'd had a row with you and she was leaving home, going to London to find her Dad. I'm not sure now she was telling me the truth,' I conceded.

'Too right,' she snapped. 'Lying little bitch.' She lit a cigarette, inhaled deeply. 'Don't get me wrong. I love her to bits. But see, she and me, we both have a temper. Lee'll tell you. She's got a vivid imagination, I'll say that,' she added. 'She sure as hell won't find her dad if that's what she's after. He's long gone.' She studied me, challenging. 'So what is it you want?'

'The school Caitlin goes to …'

'Beechwood. What about it?'

'One of the pupils there was a close friend.'

'You mean Ben. The one that killed himself. Yeah, well, it really upset her that. I mean, she's not been the same since. More secretive. She's a deep one. Always has been. Those drawings she does, give me the creeps sometimes. Makes you wonder what's going on inside her head.'

'I've seen some of her work. She is really talented.'

She shrugged. 'Got her a scholarship to that school, any road.'

'Does she have other close friends there? Someone she'd confide in?'

'Not many,' she said. 'Stuck up lot, mostly. She knew Nicky, of course,' she said. 'They used to catch the school bus together. Terrible, to think … I just thought, thank God it's not Caitlin, you know? Awful to think like that, I know, but …'

'Did she ever mention Lydia Haywood?' I asked her.

She leaned forward and stubbed out her cigarette in a heart-shaped crystal ash tray.

'Like I said. They were mostly a stuck up lot.' She glanced at her watch. I wondered again where Lee was. Out at work? Walking the dog? What if he came back now. I didn't relish the idea of him coming home and finding me there, on his territory, chatting to Caitlin's mother.

'Was Caitlin planning to do her 'A' levels at Beechwood?'

'No. She'd had enough there. I knew that, straight after Ben was found. I think she blamed the school for what happened. No, she said she wanted to go to art school in Bishops Castle. I said she'd be better off doing Maths or business studies. Damn sight more useful than art. How's she going to earn her living from art?' she said crossly. I could imagine the rows there had been over that. Couldn't entirely blame her, either. If it wasn't for my share of the business and the house we'd sold, I'd find it impossible to make a living out of my textiles.

'Did she have a Saturday job?' I asked her. 'I remember what it was like at her age, wanting to buy CDs or makeup, never having enough money.'

'She doesn't want for nothing,' she said crossly. 'Lee sees to that. Good as gold he's been with her. And what thanks does he get?' She gave a huff of indignation.

'I just wondered if she had any money of her own saved up. Money she could have taken with her.'

Her glance narrowed.

'The police asked me that. Asked if she'd been planning this disappearance.' She spoke the word as if it was a trick she was not impressed by. 'She's got a savings account, but I've no idea how much is in it.'

'What about a passport? Does she have one? Is it still here?'

'Passport? They said she's gone to London,' she said accusingly. 'You said it yourself. Gone to find her dad. What is this? Where's she gone?' she demanded crossly.

'I don't know. Not for certain,' I said.

She pulled her fingers through her curly hair in a gesture of anguish. Reaching forward, she lit another cigarette. I saw her hands were shaking. Her glance fixed on me through the pale wisp of smoke. 'The police asked me. About her passport. I couldn't find it,' she said. 'Not that it means she took it with her,' she added hastily. 'You try finding anything in her room!' She tried to sound flippant but her look was anguished, her eyes brilliant with the threat of tears. 'She could be anywhere by now. Anywhere.'

'I think I know where she's headed,' I said simply.

I left the Brooks' house just in time. As I reversed out of the drive, I saw the motorbike approaching. I accelerated away, and hoped Lee Brooks hadn't recognised my car.

I wasn't sure Caitlin's mother was reassured by my visit, but at least it gave us a focus for our search. According to her father, Lydia was in Tuscany, working in a boutique hotel in Siena. Last Monday Caitlin had taken Ben's manuscript to Beechwood School to show Dr Mackay: a piano sonata dedicated to Lydia. An exquisite piece of music that spoke eloquently of love.

'*For love of Lydia*,' I thought, remembering the book Vi had shown me. Was that why he had taken his own life? If Cat had suspected the truth before, now she was certain. Ben's long infatuation with Lydia Haywood had been hopeless. No matter how he had helped her, he would never win her over. Just how much help had he given her, I wondered then. That A star grade had taken everyone by surprise. Composition had not been her strong point. Had it all been Ben's work?

So what had really happened that day, just over a year ago, when he had taken his own life? Had he shown her the sonata he had written for her? Had she laughed at him? Her music compositions for her exams were finished. She had no further need of him. No need to flatter or befriend. Was she really so heartless she could just cut him dead. Dead … I shuddered.

'Oh, Lydia,' I murmured. 'What have you done?'

189

And now Cat knew. And knew where to find Lydia. The girl had written about her new job on Facebook, Gabriel said. I had no doubt now that Caitlin was headed for Siena in Tuscany, to confront Lydia with the truth. Was it just a confrontation, a demand for her confession? I remembered the quilt, the careful piecing, the planning, until the final paper hexagon. '*I think I have found it.*' Harriet had meticulously planned her governess's murder. Was that heritage of quiet vengeance in Caitlin's blood? What revenge would she exact for what she saw as Lydia's guilt at Ben's death?

I pulled up at the roadside. I should turn round. Go back to see Gabriel and ask if he had heard from his daughter. Was Lydia safe? I had to find him and tell him Lydia might be in danger. He had to warn her.

As I checked my mirror to pull out, I saw a motorbike approaching. I felt my stomach clench. Surely Lee Brooks hadn't followed me? I waited, only relaxing when the motorbike sped past me down the road, then I turned the car.

I headed across country for Cropstone Hall, hoping that by the time I got there, Gabriel would be back from his morning ride. Another motorbike went by. Again it startled me. I was beginning to get phobic about them. It was stupid. Of course it wasn't Lee, hot on my trail. With a distinct sense of relief I turned in at the driveway to the Hall.

There was no answer to my knock so I made my way round to the stables. I could see Monty out in the paddock. Where was Gabriel? I hadn't seen his car in the yard. I heard a scuff of noise behind me and turned. A man in cycle helmet and black leathers came towards me. Lee Brooks?

He must have followed me from his house. What had Caitlin's mother been telling him? Surely he realised I was only trying to help.

'I know where she is,' I said, my heartbeat racing. I watched as slowly he unbuckled his helmet and took it off.

'You've been poking your nose where it's not wanted,' he said. There was no smile now on that broad handsome face.

I stared from him to the horses. Had he been following me? Wasn't he just there to see to the horses. Rhiannon had told me. Keith Milford from Beechwood School. I frowned. But if he was there only for the horses, why was he so angry? Did he think I was trespassing?

'I came to find Gabriel,' I said.

'He's gone,' he said evenly. 'There's just you and me.'

I took a breath, stood my ground. I wished I'd brought William with me.

'I know where Caitlin's heading,' I said. 'I wanted to tell Gabriel. I think she's on her way to Italy to find Lydia.'

'Oh yeah?' He stood before me, too close. I could feel his breath on my face. 'What's it to do with you?'

'She blames Lydia for Ben Thomas's death,' I finished. 'But, since Gabriel's not here ...' I made to walk past him. He grabbed my arm.

'Not so fast,' he insisted. 'What do you know about her and Lydia?' he demanded.

'Only that Ben was besotted by the girl and killed himself when she rejected him.'

'You reckon?' he sneered. 'Loony, that kid. A right wimp.'

I stared at him, chin up, trying not to show how he scared me. 'You gave Caitlin a lift, didn't you? The Wednesday morning she went missing. She came here that morning, and she arranged to meet you later, up at Bury Ditches. You gave her a lift to the station.'

'So what if I did? She's all right, isn't she? You said so. On her way to Italy.'

'What did she talk about?'

'What's it to you?'

'Did she tell you she was going to Bury Ditches to put flowers on the place Ben had died? Did she tell you she blamed Lydia for Ben's death?'

'So what if she did? She had good reason, didn't she?'

'Is that what you told her?' I stared at him. What did he know about Lydia and Ben? What had he told Caitlin that morning that had made her determined to track Lydia down?'

'Caitlin's all right. You let her be. She's not like most of them stuck up bitches,' he snapped.

'Was Lydia like that? One of the stuck up bitches?'

He let out a coarse laugh. 'Liddy?' He shook his head, still grinning. 'You've got Liddy all wrong. A good healthy appetite that girl. Couldn't get enough, could she?'

I stared at him, feeling suddenly chilled. What had happened between him and Lydia? Had it to do with Ben's death?

'He idolised her. He'd written a piano sonata for her.'

'Music! What use was that to her? She wanted a real man,' Keith said, his chest puffed out.

'Is that what you told him?' I asked. 'You laughed at him. You told him to leave her alone.'

'Didn't have to, did I?' he retorted, the smile hardening in his face. 'He saw us. Just stood there, watching us.'

I frowned. 'At the school?'

'I'm not that stupid!' he said. He dragged me by the arm towards the stables, pulled open the door and pushed me inside. 'Here, we were here. At it. You know?' he said, his face thrust close into mine. 'She liked it out here. I liked her just about anywhere. Such an arse on her,' he said with a leer. His bulk in the doorway dimmed the light. I felt sick, scared. What had happened? What had he done?

'On study leave, she was. She was a boarder during the week, but she liked to come back here, get away from school. Got her own car, hadn't she? Daddy's birthday present to his little girl. I was grooming Monty. We'd been out for a ride. And there she was, her blouse open, no bra, her hands all over me. So we go at it. And I just looked up and there was the kid, standing in the doorway, just staring at us, some book in his hand. I pulled back so he could get a real good look at her, see what a great pair of tits she had. See what he was missing. And I never missed a beat, you know? We were laughing and it really felt good. Turned her on like I'd never seen her before. When we'd finished, he was gone. Next I heard, he'd topped himself.' His hand touched my shoulder, traced down my arm. 'She went away after that. But there's plenty of others to take her place. A string of keen young fillies.'

'Like Nicky Price?' I suggested, my mouth dry.

'What do you know about Nicky?' he demanded, the anger gleaming in his eyes. He held my arms with bruising fingers.

'Did you try it on with her?'

'There was nothing between us, Nicky and me, you got that?' he said, jabbing a finger at my chest.

'OK, OK.'

Still he did not let go of me, but it seemed as if there were two warring urges within him. Neither of them had my welfare in mind. 'What happened with Nicky then?'

'I never meant to!' he blurted out.

I stared at him, hardly breathing. 'You killed her?'

'She'd finished a late shift at the supermarket. I saw her walking home and stopped to give her a lift. I only touched her, you know. Friendly, like. And she laughed.' His eyes widened as if the anger he had felt that night still raged within him. 'Laughed, she did.'

'The way you and Lydia had laughed at Ben?' I suggested.

'She shouldn't have laughed,' he said bleakly. 'I just wanted her to shut up.' His face crumpled with a tight frown, raking over the memories. 'She said some stuff about Liddy. About how she'd make fun of me, riding round on her father's horses like I was the Lord of the Manor instead of just some loser. It wasn't true. Liddy wouldn't never have said that. We were special, me and Liddy. She'd never have said that about me!' he said, growing angry again.

'Said what?' I prompted.

'She said Liddy … Liddy used to call me her local yokel. She said as how I was all right if you didn't mind the stink of horse shit. And she laughed at me. I … I dunno … I put my hands up to her face. Tried to shut her up. And she did. And then she wasn't breathing no more,' he finished, his eyes filled with anguish. 'She shouldn't have laughed.' He focused on me more intently then. 'You see where she's brought me? What she's made me do?' he said.

194

'You have to go to the police. You have to tell them what happened,' I said as firmly as I could, fighting to control the tremble of fear through my body. I had to calm him, make him see sense. I was afraid of what he would do next. 'Keith, you must let me go. Before it's too late.'

But he was shaking his head, all the while I was talking.

'No!' he burst out. 'I can't! I can't let them lock me away. You do see that?'

'Keith, please, let me go.'

His head swung slowly from side to side, all the while his gaze drilled into me.

'It's not my fault, do you see? If you hadn't gone on asking questions. Rhiannon told me you'd been asking about me.' He turned and grabbed for the spade that stood against the wall and swung it at me. Somehow I ducked in time but it caught me on the side of my head. I screamed out in pain, but then the blackness overcame me.

'Love for Lydia,' Vi said with a sigh. 'I think, in his way, Keith Milford really did love her. She made him feel special.'

'Until Nicky undermined everything he believed in.'

'Just like poor Ben.'

'Just like Ben,' I echoed, and winced.

'How's the head?'

'Don't ask.' I closed my eyes.

I had woken to find myself in a shaded hospital room, and within hours Vi had come to tell me about Keith's arrest. Looking round, the room seemed filled with flowers. Their fragrance filled the room. Lilies, roses, carnations, orchids. A rainbow of colours. And most of them from Gabriel Haywood.

'OK if I come in? They said I could have two minutes.'

I squinted towards the doorway and saw Gabriel standing there, bearing more roses. Why had he sent all those flowers? To assuage his guilt at what Lydia had done?

'Thanks for the flowers,' I said.

'A bouquet every day,' Vi said.

'Then … how long?' I croaked.

'Four days,' Gabriel said, his voice gravelly. 'I thought we were going to lose you.'

'Vi said you were a hero. So what happened?'

'You don't remember?'

I didn't even try shaking my head.

'He came back and found you in a heap in the straw,' Vi said. She glanced up at Gabriel. She gave a knowing smile and patted my hand. 'I'll go and find another vase,' she said and retreated.

'Keith said you'd gone.'

'I was on my way to the airport. I rang Keith to ask him to see to the horses. I didn't know how long I'd be away.'

'Lydia!' I remembered in sudden panic the reason for my mission to Cropstone Hall.

'She rang me, quite distraught. Caitlin showed up at the hotel that morning, accusing her of murder. She was scared. She didn't know what to do. There was a flight to Milan at midday. It was tight, but I reckoned I could make Birmingham airport in time. I was going to ring you when I got there to let you know Caitlin had turned up. I only got as far as Bridgnorth and realised I'd left my passport in the safe so I had to turn round and come back. Luckily. I saw your car in drive and heard voices. I'm only sorry I didn't get there sooner.

As soon as Keith saw me, he legged it. He grabbed Monty and took off. He's a good rider, but bareback …' He gave a shake of his head, a voluble wince. 'That high gate into the village got him. Monty refused and he sailed over. Broke his leg. The police nabbed him. He's safe behind bars now,' he reassured me.

'He hated the thought of being locked up,' I said.

'Good. He deserves to suffer.'

I frowned. 'But what about Caitlin?'

'She's home safe,' he said. 'Her stepdad flew out there and brought her home yesterday. Seems she's done some thinking on her travels. She's going back to Beechwood to sit her exams, then it's art school next autumn.'

'I'm glad,' I said, and smiled rather gingerly. My mouth hurt. I took a breath.

'And Lydia? How is she?'

'Shaken. But she'll survive. I don't think she'd realised until then the pain she'd caused.'

'Did she tell you anything about her music 'A' level?'

'We did discuss it last year,' he said evenly. His glance dipped away from me. I knew he felt guilty. 'Ben did help her, more than a little. But what good will it do now to make a fuss? At least Ben's music has counted for something. And Lydia's learned her lesson, I think.'

'So she's still set on Oxford?' I said, angry that the girl had sailed through everyone's disasters unscathed. Ben was dead, Nicky murdered, yet Lydia's gilded life went on almost unshadowed.

'Oh yes. I hope she dazzles the dons. For Ben's sake. It'd be a pity to think all his hard work was for nothing.'

I glared at him, even more angry that Gabriel could still so proud of his daughter.

'After all she's done? The havoc she's wreaked?'

'What would you have me do?' he countered. 'Send her to a nunnery? Cut her off without a penny?' He gave a deep sigh. 'It's my fault, don't you see? I should have been there for her when she was growing up,' he said in anguish. 'I was always so busy, chasing the next deal, too busy to fly back for her birthday. It was easier just to sign a bigger cheque. So much for my parental guidance.'

'You should have got a governess for her,' I snapped. And instantly regretted it. On reflection, the way things had turned out, I doubted the Dash family had fared much better.

He sank his head into his hands.

'What a mess. What a bloody mess,' he groaned. 'Ben. Nicky. Caitlin ...'

'At least Lydia has escaped unharmed,' I said coldly.

He stared at me, his eyes darkened.

'Is that really what you think?' he said, his voice strained. He got to his feet. 'It's time I went. I'm tiring you. I'm glad you're on the mend.'

I shut my eyes. I was still aching, my head thudded. Now was not the time to take it out on Gabriel. Lydia was eighteen, after all. Old enough to make her own decisions. Her own mistakes. And face the consequences. Whatever Caitlin had said to her in Italy had obviously frightened her. Perhaps I shouldn't have been quite so hard on Gabriel. I could see in his eyes that he bitterly regretted all that had happened.

'Sorry,' I said weakly, but when I opened my eyes he had gone. Vi stood there holding an empty vase, her gaze quizzical.

'I don't know why you're blaming yourself,' she said briskly.

I sighed. I'd been trying for so long not to think about Ed, about the car park. Something in the way Gabriel had looked at me brought it all horribly back: a father's fierce pride in his daughter, an unquestioning love, that instinct to defend, as strong as any maternal instinct. 'You've no idea,' I said at last.

'Then perhaps you should tell me,' she said, settling into the chair at my bedside.

So I did.

Vi, like a confessor, listened patiently, nodding wisely, though I very much doubted if my feelings and experience mirrored anything in her own life. Vi was not that stupid.

'That Autumn was bloody awful,' I said. 'Ed had moved out. There was the business to untangle. I could hardly go on working with him. I knew where she lived, and knew Ed was with her and the baby. So I took to sitting in the car, just across the road from their house, watching the lights go on and off, watching them go out, come home. So happy together. And I had nothing and no-one.'

'He saw you there?'

'He must have done. He'd have recognised the car.'

'So what happened?'

'Christmas,' I said.

'Ah.' I could hear it in her voice: recognition of the isolation I had felt. While everyone else was playing happy families, I was alone, an outsider. Every jangling carol and TV advert blared out the message: Christmas is a time for children, a celebration of the family. And Ed with his new wife and baby were in the thick of it all. I was jealous. I'd been waiting, year after year, for the time we could be together as a family for the first time, with a child of our own. Well, he'd succeeded. But where did that leave me? Out in the cold. Literally. Bloody freezing in that car,' I said, with a lopsided smile. Not that I felt much like smiling when I remembered.

'The week before Christmas, I followed her. Wasn't the first time. This time she drove to the shopping mall, her and the baby. The traffic was snarled up but she got a parking space. Mother and Baby. I had to park some way off. I should have gone home then, but something in me just wouldn't let go. I had to find her. I thought I'd lost her, but then, there she was, in a bookshop. I went in and pretended to be looking for something on the shelves, but I wanted to see the baby. Ed's baby. It was asleep in the pushchair. Its face was goblet shaped, and its cheeks were red and shiny, like a tulip. Not a pretty child. I was glad.'

'Teething, probably,' Vi said mildly.

'I remember hoping it kept him awake with its crying. Anyway, she didn't seem to notice me, so when she left the shop, I followed her. There were crowds everywhere, and those awful raucous carols. It was really hard for her to make her way round. I kept thinking, what if she leaves the pushchair outside the shop? What if I took the child? I mean, not to keep, just to show she wasn't the perfect mother Ed thought her.'

Vi said nothing, but I sensed her stiffen. I saw her hands clench a little tighter on the arm of the chair.

'Then she was heading for the exit, walking fast. There were carrier bags swinging on the handles of the pushchair. It was hard for her, steering her way through, out to the car park.' I could picture her even now, a slight figure, bowed against the darkness and the sleet on the wind. She had no scarf or umbrella. She just kept pushing the pushchair, head down, until she reached her car. 'She was unloading her shopping into the boot,' I said. 'The baby started crying. She looked tired and cold. I thought she was going to burst into tears. Then she caught sight of me. "What do you want?" she said. "You've been following me. I saw you!" and her face was hot and red like the tulip's, and the baby only cried all the more loudly. And I stood there, feeling stupid. "I'm Ed's wife," I said. She glared at me, her mouth thin and angry. "Not any more," she said, and slammed the boot shut. Then she opened the car door and caught up the baby in its chair and strapped it into the back seat. Then she grabbed the pushchair frame to fold it up. Only she'd forgotten one of the bags and it upended onto the tarmac into the wet slush. I looked down and saw it was a plant book. One I knew Ed had wanted. She'd been out to buy his Christmas present. And I just stood there, staring, while the book got wet and the spine was cracked. And I couldn't stop crying.'

'I'm sorry,' Vi said softly. 'You should have talked to someone. Told them how you felt. They could have helped you.'

'No-one could have helped me,' I said fiercely. 'I had to learn that it was over. That she was the one who would give him all he needed from now on.'

'Did you see him again after that?'

'Oh yes,' I said, my cheeks heating at the memory. 'He was bloody furious when she got back and told him what had happened. He came round to the house. Threatened me. If I did anything like that again, he'd go to the police. He told me I'd got to get on with my life. As if he had nothing to do with the chaos I was in!'

'I suppose he had a right to be angry. He was just protecting his family.'

201

'His family, yes, exactly,' I said bitterly. Then sighed. 'It's OK. I'm over it now. I hate to think what he'd have done if he'd known I'd thought of taking the child. I was so angry with him. I hated him for what he'd made me do.'

'But you survived,' Vi said.

I nodded. 'Thanks to the quilts. I was in a coffee bar. Feeling sorry for myself as usual. Wondering what Ed and the tulip were doing. There was an exhibition on. Patchwork quilts. It was as if a light had been switched on, after I'd been living in the dark for so long. Seeing the pieces joined together, creating a story, a pattern, it suddenly made sense to me. I knew what I wanted to do with my life. I had all the pieces of the past, but they didn't fit together properly. I realised I could still shape my future, create something I wanted, something I could be proud of.'

Vi smiled.

'I'm so glad you did,' she said. She reached out and took my hand and gently squeezed it.

'Sometimes salvation comes on four legs,' she confided. And in the glance we exchanged, I guessed that not all of my story was as alien to her as I had supposed. One day, she might tell me, I thought.

Across the grass the notes of music drifted serenely, hovering over the placid waters of the lake, swirling up into the trees along the ridgeway track. In spotted bow tie and silk waistcoat, Dr Mackay conducted his string quintet as the guests emerged from the exhibition marquee to stroll through the walled garden and across the lawn. Vi had dug out one of her floaty chiffon dresses from a bygone era she said had been her Isadora Duncan phase.

'So much better than that dreadful garden party I came to once,' she said, reaching for another glass of champagne. 'In this light, Cropstone looks enchanting. What a place to live! If you hadn't already staked a claim on Gabriel, I'd be after him myself.'

'Vi, I haven't!' I began protesting. 'In fact, I haven't forgiven him. The way he's given in to Lydia time and again. She thinks she can get away with …' I hesitated. 'With anything she wants,' I finished lamely. Murder was the last thing I wanted to evoke on such a beautiful celebratory evening.

Vi patted my arm.

'You mustn't be too hard on him,' she whispered. 'He's a very kind and loving father. And very generous. You can't really hate him for that, can you?'

I pulled a face.

'I could try.'

'The quilts look terrific,' Caitlin said as she came to find us.

'Thanks,' I said, and smiled at her. Her GCSEs over, she looked calmer, almost relaxed, her Goth make-up softened by the glow from the champagne that flushed her cheeks pink.

'This time next year, it'll be your pictures on show,' Vi said.

'Don't think Cropstone is quite ready for Urban Noir,' she said with a giggle.

Inside the marquee the stands were hung with the four art quilts of trees, finished at last thanks to a desperate burst of machining, stitching and beading over the past three weeks. Irena had displayed a selection of my smaller patchwork and textile pieces in frames on the panels opposite. I was relieved to see there were already a few red dots against the pieces, which had been sold.

Pride of place in the marquee was given to the Dash family quilt, displayed together with the little silver pin box. Caitlin had suggested we put up a floral display to echo the plants Harriet had pictured in her quilt. I told her I didn't think the hemlock and deadly nightshade mixed well with the canapés. You had to be so careful these days with Health and Safety. But Cat's presentation of a potted history of the Dash family, as far as she had been able to research, had been a delight. And unexpected.

'I found out more about them,' she had told me when she came to visit me after I came home from hospital. 'At least, about my great-great-grandparents.'

'How come? We couldn't find any trace of Harriet after 1881.'

Cat smiled.

'Not Harriet,' she said. 'When I got back from Italy, I told Mum what we'd found out. She dug out Nan's stuff. Photo albums. Certificates. She'd pushed them all in a box in the loft after Nan died. But there were marriage certificates, birth certificates, the lot. There was even an old family Bible, and someone, my great-great-great-grandma we think, had listed the names of all the children that were born, and all their marriages. We went through it all together. I think Mum really got a kick out of it. A bit of mother daughter bonding,' she said, trying to sound cynical, but her smile betrayed the experience had not been unwelcome.

'You found Harriet?'

Cat shook her head.

'I told you. Not Harriet. There was a death certificate for my great-grandma Kate's mother. I looked her up on the internet. On the 1911 census she

204

was a widow living with her son and daughter-in-law. That's Grandma Kate's parents. Her name was Gwen Hughes. I found her marriage on that website you showed me. She was married in August 1881 to James Hughes. He was a clerk on the railway, it said. Her maiden name was Lloyd.'

'Gwen Lloyd? Harriet's nanny? You're sure?'

'Positive. I got Mum to send for her birth certificate and the marriage certificate. I reckon Harriet gave her the quilt as a wedding present.'

'So what happened to Harriet?' I asked, bewildered.

Cat shrugged.

'Don't think we'll ever know,' she said. 'Reckon she went abroad, like you said, and married there.'

'Canapés?' Rhiannon asked, edging towards us through the crowed with a silver tray of dainty pastries and blinis.

'This is just gorgeous,' I told her, nibbling one of the tiny crab tarts. She smiled broadly.

'It seems to be going down well. I've already had a couple of enquiries for party catering.'

'Clive looks pleased,' Vi said.

'He came to see me in hospital and most magnanimously told me he'd forgiven me for telling the police he'd taken Caitlin to Bury Ditches. He said he understood I had acted with the highest of motives.'

Vi giggled. 'You mean all the notoriety the case had brought you means there's suddenly a lot of interest in your work.'

'I suppose for forty per cent commission he can afford to be forgiving,' I conceded.

I wasn't entirely sure who had come up with the idea of exhibiting at Cropstone Hall. Clive had insisted that, with all the publicity over the Milford case, his gallery space in Ludlow was not big enough. Vi said it was Gabriel's idea, as a way of making amends to me, on Libby's behalf. Either way, it was an inspired choice. Cropstone Hall had never looked more tranquil or more beautiful, assuaging the terrifying memory I had of Keith's attack on me.

'Of course we'll never know for certain what happened to Harriet Dash or her governess,' I heard Gabriel telling the rapt little party around him as I made my way out of the marquee. 'That much is still Cropstone's own mystery.'

I strolled down towards the lake and paused to look back at the house, sipping champagne. I realised I had not thought of Ed in days. Not conjured his face, grinning at me through armfuls of pot plants. Not reached out in bed for him. Not even, thankfully, remembered his look of utter fury when he found out I'd been stalking his new wife. Perhaps Vi was right. Cropstone did have its own enchantment, its own spell to weave. Just like the power of the patchwork, I felt I had finally managed to piece my life back together again.

It was good to know Caitlin was safe, and that Lydia was apparently contrite. I even thought Mrs Thomas had looked a little more at peace than I'd seen her the last time we'd met, and wondered if it had anything to do with Dr Mackay's soothing Scots lilt.

'Do you think she'd approve?' Cat asked as she caught up with me and slipped her arm through mine. 'Harriet, having her quilt on display like that. She was such a secretive person.'

'It was how she expressed herself, I suppose. It's not easy for some people to communicate what they're really feeling.'

Cat nodded in silence. She was thinking of Ben. We both were. She gave a sigh.

'I wish we could have met her.'

'Her art has survived. It is a beautiful quilt,' I said.

'So what are you planning next?' she asked me, her face tilted up, all the bright confidence and hope restored to her eyes.

I glanced back at the marquee and saw Gabriel watching us. He gave a slight nod, his lips forming a hesitant smile. Was he forgiven?

I sighed. On such an evening, with the rosy sun casting gilded beams across the lake, the swallows swooping low over the grass, and that sense of peace and promise enveloping us, it would take a stonier heart than mine to resist. I smiled, and raised my glass in thanks.

8

HARRIET

Weighing a good thirty pounds more than she felt comfortable with, and on the wrong side of fifty, Harry stood on the gravel drive, shading her eyes as she stared up at the house.

'Wow, isn't that something?' she said, her accent a languid American drawl.

'C'mon, honey. We got to get going. Someone might come and chuck us off.'

'There's no-one in, sweetheart. I knocked. Just wait a minute, will you? I want to take a picture. My people used to live here years ago.'

Tom sighed and got out of the rental car.

'So you said.'

'It's true!' she protested. 'I did the research online. Cropstone Hall. This is it.'

'OK, OK. Go on. Stand on the steps then, like you own the place,' he said, his smile indulgent.

'So who were these grandparents of yours anyway? Lords and ladies?'

'I guess not. And they were my great-great-grandparents. They came over to the States in the 1880s. Remember that silver thimble I got? Mom gave it me when I was twenty-one. It used to belong to great-great-grandma Harriet. I'm named for her.'

'A thimble? What the hell's a thimble?' he muttered, checking the satnav. 'Come on. We'll be late for the concert.'

Harry smiled, and one last time turned and looked up at the grand house.

'It's a shame there's no-one's at home. I'd have liked to look round the place. See where she lived. It's so beautiful here. She must really have missed it.'

'And we'll miss the concert if we don't get going. Says it's thirteen miles to Ludlow, but you know what these skinny lanes are like. Probably take us an hour to find the goddam place.'

Harry clambered back into the car, watching over her shoulder all the while as they bumped back down the drive.

'It's for sewing,' she said.

'What is?'

'The thimble,' she said. 'It protects your finger when you pull the needle through a quilt,' she explained, waggling her plump fingers at him. He made a grab for them, laughing, and closed his lips around them. Harriet Kendall smiled. Tom had never understood her passion for quilting. But his passion for her was never in doubt.

THE END

FURTHER INFORMATION

The inspiration for this story came from a Victorian patchwork quilt I saw at the Quilt Association's exhibition at the Minerva Art Centre in 2009: a hexagon top with papers. It was just one of many beautiful quilts in their collection of mainly Welsh quilts from the Llanidloes and mid Wales area.

The railway line between Craven Arms and Bishops Castle opened in 1865 but always struggled for funding. Only two sides of planned triangular route were completed, so engines had to reverse at Lydham Heath to take the carriages on to Bishops Castle.

The poem from which the quotation '*to beauty sacred, and those angel eyes*' is taken is '*To his Sleeping Mistress*' by John Fletcher (1579-1625), the playwright who, with Francis Beaumont, wrote the bawdy comedy 'The Knight of the Burning Pestle'.

> *Oh, fair sweet face! oh, eyes, celestial bright,*
> *Twin stars in heaven, that now adorn the night!*
> *Oh, fruitful lips, where cherries ever grow,*
> *And damask cheeks, where all sweet beauties blow!*
> *Oh, thou, from head to foot divinely fair!*
> *Cupid's most cunning net's made of that hair;*
> *And, as he weaves himself for curious eyes,*
> *"Oh me, oh me, I'm caught myself!" he cries:*
> *Sweet rest about thee, sweet and golden sleep,*
> *Soft peaceful thoughts, your hourly watches keep,*
> *Whilst I in wonder sing this sacrifice,*
> *To beauty sacred, and those angel eyes!*

ACKNOWLEDGEMENTS

In researching plant poisons for this book, I have read and enjoyed the wealth of plant knowledge and folklore in John Robertson's book, *'Is that cat dead: and other questions about poison plants'* available in paperback and as a kindle ebook. I also found informative and entertaining Kathryn Hughes' excellent book, *'The Victorian Governess'*.

My thanks to my editor, Fran, at Powers-Gardiner Publishing Services for casting her beady eye over the text, and for her advice. Who knew she had the gift to detect the smell of cyanide?

FORTY MOTIFS

The following motifs feature in the patchwork quilt. The templates can be photocopied and resized for your own art projects. You can also download the templates as PDFs or as cutting files in Silhouette Studio and Craft Robo GSD software, from my website at:

www.beanpolebooks.co.uk/QD1_40motifs.html

These template designs are my copyright. Please do not copy and share or sell the templates without my written permission.

APPLE SEEDS

BASS CLEF

BELL

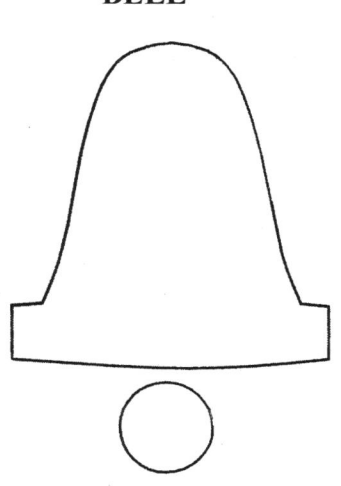

213

BLUEBELL

BUTTERCUP

214

CUCKOO PINT

CYCLAMEN

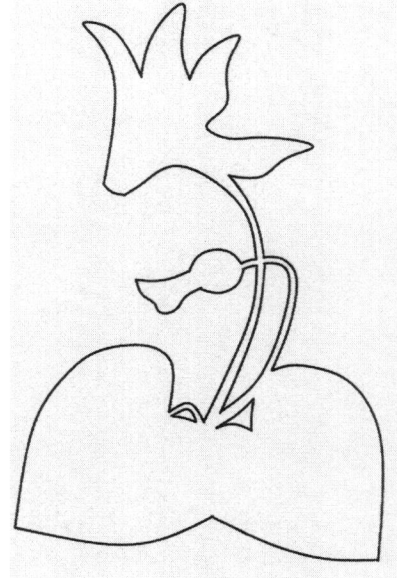

215

DAISY

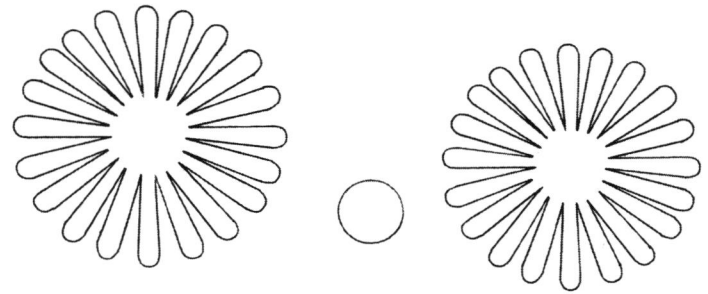

DAFFODIL

DEADLY NIGHTSHADE

FERN

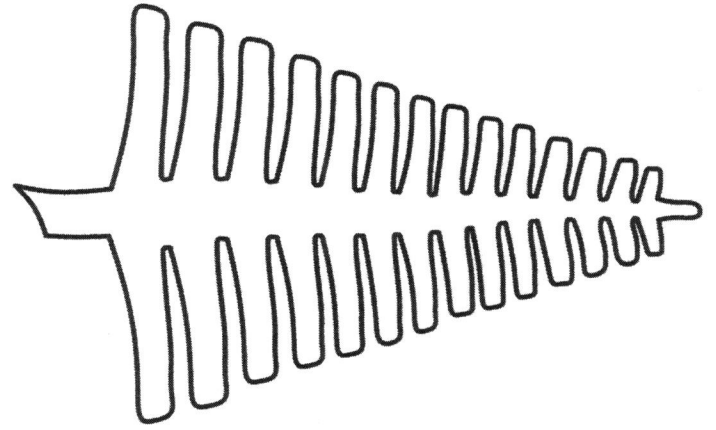

FORGET ME NOT

FOXGLOVE

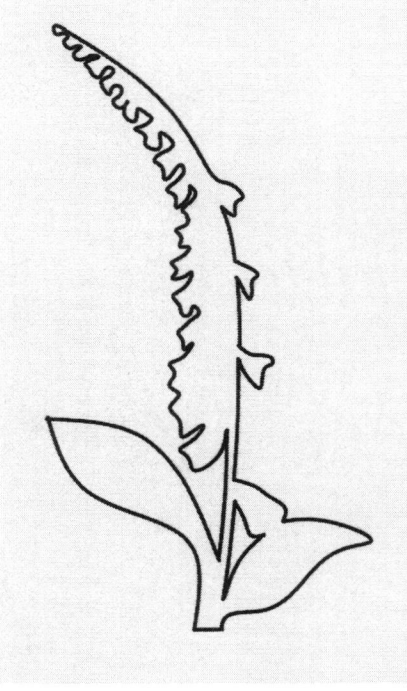

218

HEART

HELLEBORE
flower

leaf

HEMLOCK

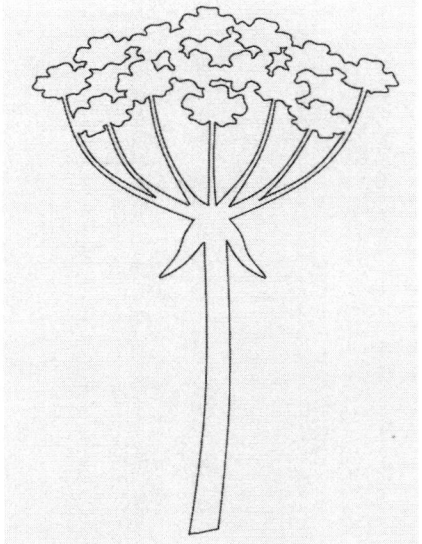

HOLLY

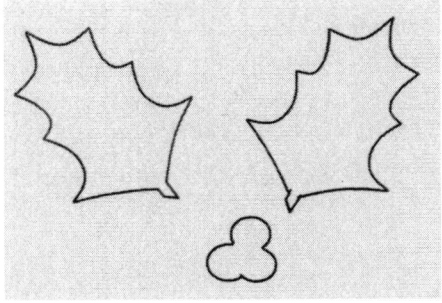

HOLLYHOCK

IVY

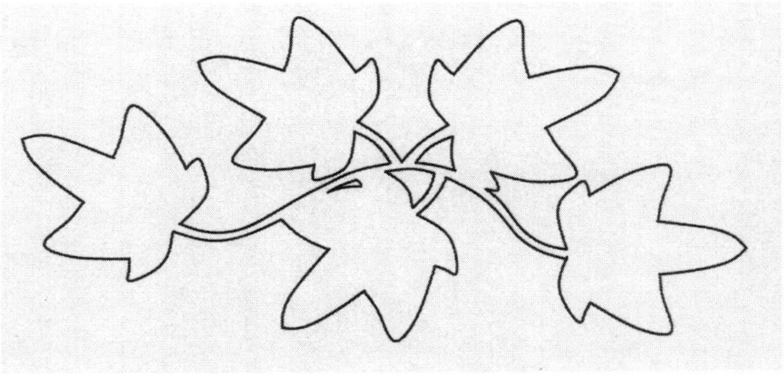

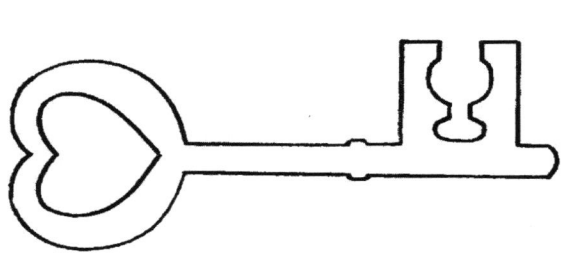

KEY

LABURNUM

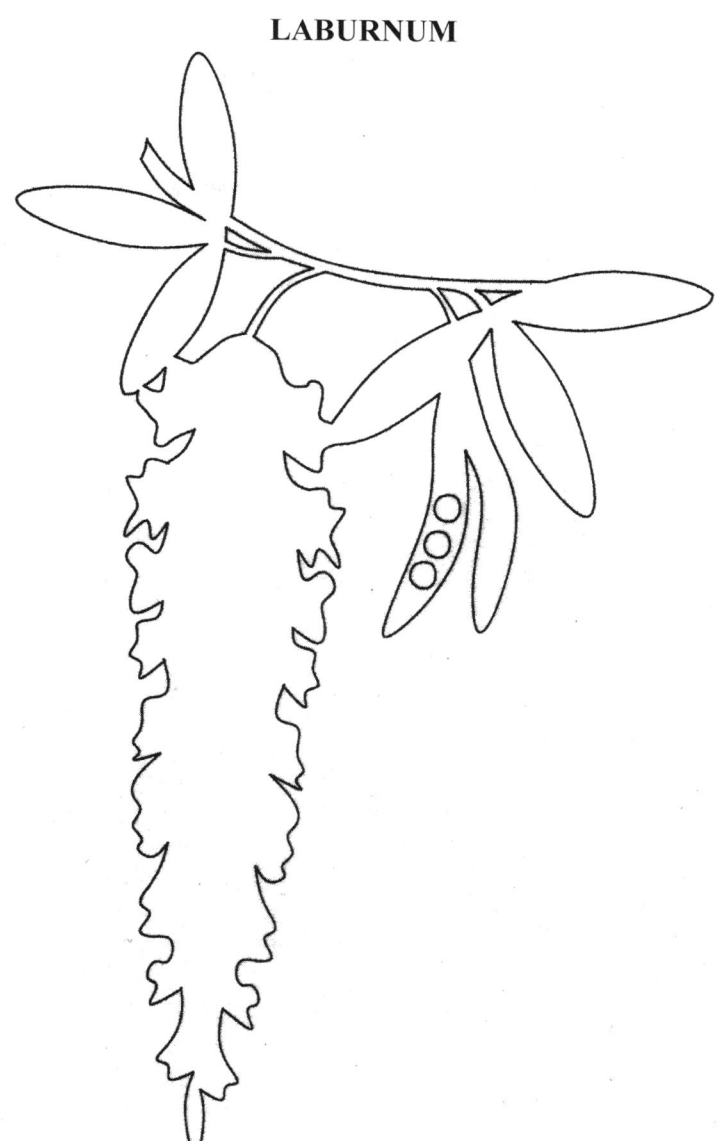

LAUREL

LAVENDER

224

LILY OF THE VALLEY

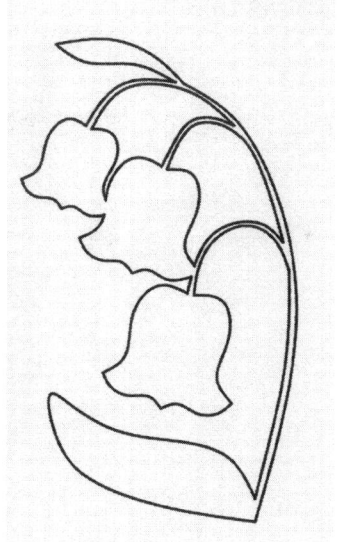

MISTLETOE

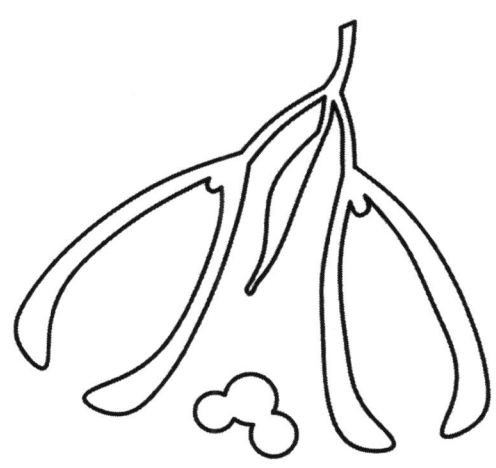

MONKSHOOD

OAK LEAF

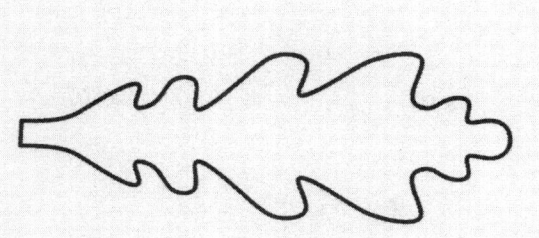

PALM LEAF

PEONY

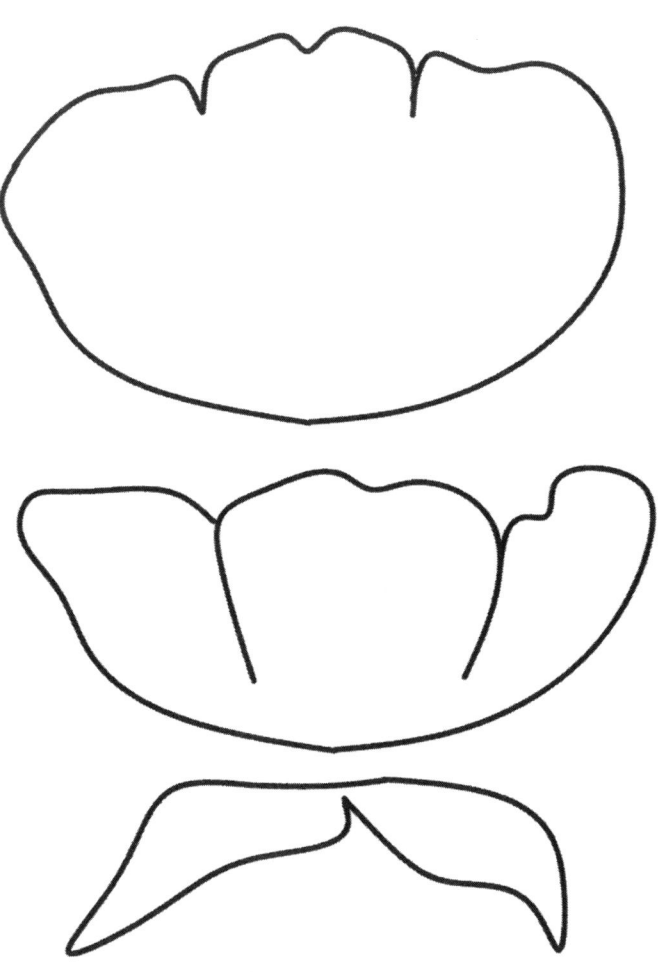

POPPY

PRIMROSE

QUAVER

ROSE LEAF

ROSE

SNOWDROP

SWEET PEA

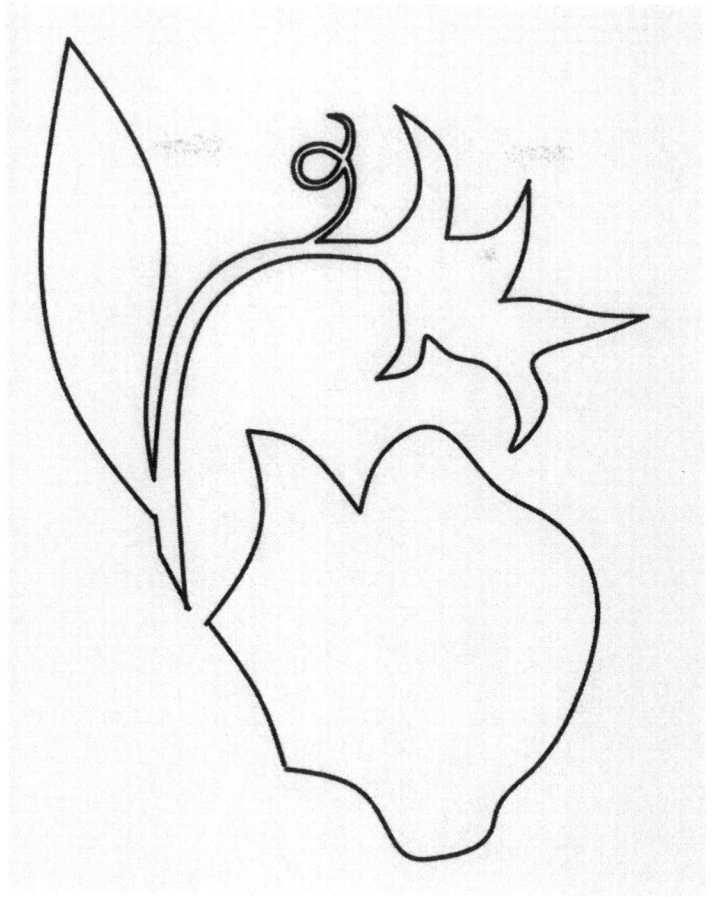

TREBLE CLEF

TULIP

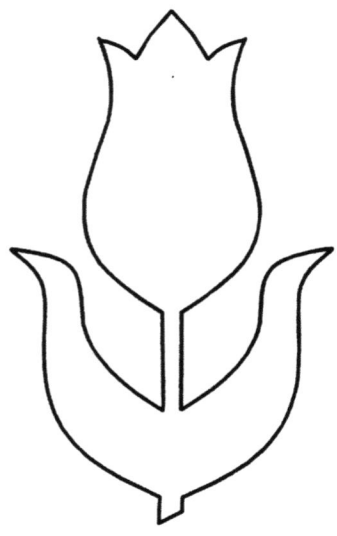

VIOLET

WHITE BRYONY

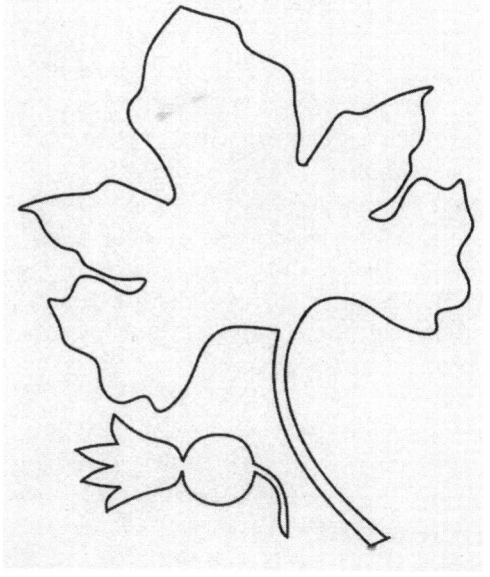

Also by Karen Lowe:

STAR GARDENS SERIES

DEATH IN THE PHYSIC GARDEN

Amazon reviews:
'well written with a complex plot and some interesting characters'
'I enjoyed this so much that I immediately bought the next in the series'
'Excellent writing. Good storytelling'
'This mystery features some beautiful description and heaps of gardening knowledge, as well as a gritty murder puzzle and a difficult, but promising relationship that begins to develop in this first book of what surely will be a series. For the discerning reader'
Readers reviews:
'the atmosphere and location are brilliantly done'
'marvellous flower detail'
'I never guessed the ending'

Death in the Physic Garden introduces garden designer Fern Green who has escaped from London and her abusive boyfriend to find refuge in the remote South Shropshire hills. Setting up her garden design business, Star Gardens, she believes she has found peace and safety at last until she discovers the body of her first client, wealthy herbalist Joshua Hamble, dead in his physic garden. As she becomes ensnared in the Hambles' family secrets, she unearths a trail of murder and revenge. As DI Drummond warns her, 'Gardening can be a dangerous business.'

Read an extract at www.beanpolebooks.co.uk

Order online from www.beanpolebooks.co.uk
or from Amazon as a Kindle download
ISBN-13: 978-0953177042

DEATH IN THE WINTER GARDEN
Karen Lowe

2011 Quarter Finalist,
Amazon Breakthrough Novel Award

Amazon reviews
'This is so well-written!'
'I loved everything about this excerpt - from the setting (the damp, rainy countryside, and let's not forget the potentially beautiful gardens), to the sense of loss woven throughout the excerpt, and then to the characters...There is a wonderful sense of familiarity here as well, I instantly felt like I could know the characters, which made me invest in them right away. Excellent'
'If you like your crime novels cosy with an unusual background then I would recommend this book and its predecessor, Death in the Physic Garden'
'More gorgeous gardening from the talented and capable Fern Green. I fell in love with her in the previous book (Death in the Physic Garden), and this time around that love deepened. An enjoyable read'

'Death in the Winter Garden' continues Fern Green's career, and her relationship with hunky Welsh detective, DI Ross Drummond. When the body of a newborn baby is found in the long-neglected garden of Plas Graig, Fern discovers that the secrets of the past still haunt the living. When a girl is murdered in nearby woods, the echoes of past wrongs can no longer be stifled. But Fern soon discovers that there are some in the village who would prefer the past remained buried. As she tries to find a link with an apparent suicide six years before, her quest to unearth the truth puts her own life in danger.

Order online from www.beanpolebooks.co.uk
or from Amazon as a Kindle download
ISBN-13: 978-0953177059

7305373R00129

Made in the USA
San Bernardino, CA
31 December 2013